国内独家授权，全球热销上亿册

双语
精华版

心灵鸡汤

[经典系列]

光阴的故事--

王少凯　杨晓阳　译

As Time Goes by

Jack Canfield & Mark Victor Hansen 等　著

Chicken
Soup for the
Soul

安徽科学技术出版社
Health Communications, Inc.

图书在版编目(CIP)数据

心灵鸡汤:双语精华版. 光阴的故事/(美)坎费尔德(Canfield,J.)等著;王少凯,杨晓阳译. —合肥:安徽科学技术出版社,2007.8
ISBN 978-7-5337-3879-2

Ⅰ. 心… Ⅱ.①坎…②王…③杨… Ⅲ.①英语-汉语-对照读物②故事-作品集-美国-现代 Ⅳ.H319.4:Ⅰ

中国版本图书馆 CIP 数据核字(2007)第 129498 号

心灵鸡汤:双语精华版. 光阴的故事
(美)坎费尔德(Canfield,J.)等著 王少凯 杨晓阳译

出 版 人:朱智润
责任编辑:李瑞生
封面设计:王国亮
出版发行:安徽科学技术出版社(合肥市政务文化新区圣泉路 1118 号
　　　　　出版传媒广场,邮编:230071)
电　　话:(0551)3533330
网　　址:www.ahstp.com.cn
E - mail:yougoubu@sina.com
经　　销:新华书店
排　　版:安徽事达科技贸易有限公司
印　　刷:合肥华云印务有限公司
开　　本:889×1100　1/24
印　　张:10
字　　数:202 千
版　　次:2007 年 8 月第 1 版　2007 年 8 月第 1 次印刷
印　　数:10 000
定　　价:25.00 元

(本书如有印装质量问题,影响阅读,请向本社市场营销部调换)

作为原生于美国的大众心理自助与人生励志类的闪亮品牌,《心灵鸡汤》语言地道新颖,优美流畅,极富时代感。书中一个个叩人心扉的故事,充分挖掘平凡小事所蕴藏的精神力量和人性之美,真率倾诉对生命的全新体验和深层感悟,字里行间洋溢着爱心、感恩、信念、鼓励和希望。因其内涵哲思深邃,豁朗释然,央视"百家讲坛"曾引用其作为解读援例。

文本适读性与亲和力、故事的吸引力和感召力、内涵的人文性和震撼力,煲出了鲜香润泽的《心灵鸡汤》——发行40多个国家和地区,总销量达一亿多册的全球超级畅销书!

安徽科学技术出版社独家引进的该系列英文版,深得广大读者的推崇与青睐,频登各大书店及"开卷市场零售监测系统"的畅销书排行榜,多次荣获全国出版发行业的各类奖项。

就学英语而言,本系列读物的功效已获广大读者乃至英语教学界的充分肯定。由于书中文章的信度和效度完全符合大规模标准化考试对考题的质量要求,全国大学英语四级考试、全国成人高考的阅读理解真题曾采用其中的文章。大学英语通用教材曾采用其中的文章作为精读课文。

为了让更多读者受惠于这一品牌,我社又获国内独家授权,隆重推出双语精华版《心灵鸡汤》系列:英汉美文并蓄、双语同一视面对照——广大读者既能在轻松阅读中提高英语水平,又能从中感悟人生的真谛,激发你搏击风雨、奋发向上的生命激情!

CONTENTS

目 录

目 录

2

Never Give Up
永不放弃

What we do today,right now,will have an accumulated effect on all our tomorrows.

Alexandra Stoddard

今天所做的事情会对明天产生累积的影响。

亚历山德拉·史达德尔

At twenty-three,Chad's life was just beginning.Handsome and popular,he had been a long-distance runner and a top wrestler in school and was still pursued by young women of all descriptions.People who met Chad couldn't help but like him instantly.He had a wide,infectious smile,brimmed with good humor and was the sort of person who would drop everything at a moment's notice to help out a friend.

He had purchased the motorcycle to have transportation to the

23岁,查德的生活刚刚开始。他是学校长跑选手和摔跤高手,外表英俊,惹人喜爱,受到各种年轻女人的追捧。只要见到他,人们就会情不自禁为其吸引。他性情开朗,笑容富有感染力,是那种毫不犹豫、倾心帮助朋友的人。

为住更好的公寓、买车和家具,查德干了两份工作,为了做这两

two jobs he held.Working two jobs would help him save for a better apartment and maybe a car and some furniture of his own.But one night on his way to job number two,a drunk driver,who carried no insurance, careened into him,spilling the bike and shattering Chad's leg.Now,at twenty-three,his life seemed to be ending.

For seven agonizing months,Chad lay in a hospital bed,staring at the metal framework of skewers that penetrated his leg at several points, holding it together.Pieces of his bone had been left in the street,and Chad went through operation after operation in a vain attempt to save the leg from amputation.His friends organized blood drives for Chad's operations,and his supervisors at work held his job open for him in hopes he would be able to return to work.

When the doctors announced the leg had to come off,Chad sank into a bitter despair.How would he function with only one leg?Would he become repulsive to women and never marry or have the family he had always dreamed of?And how would he ever find a way to pay the hospital bills that had now soared to the cost of a new three-bedroom house?

Nothing we did cheered Chad or eased his deep depression,as we waited for his bone infection to be cured before the leg was amputated.It would not be good to undergo such an operation with Chad not caring if he survived it.

One night,I brought the husband of a colleague of mine at work to Chad's hospital room.Gene began talking at once,joking with Chad, telling him he was "on his last leg" and he "only had one leg to stand on."

Chad was furious."How can you come into my room and talk like that when they're going to cut off my leg?" he demanded to know.

Gene just shrugged.Then he bent over,unbuckled his own leg and threw the prosthesis on Chad's bed.I left them alone.

份工作,他还买了摩托车。一天夜里,在他上第2份班的途中,一个没上保险、醉酒的司机开着飞车,歪歪斜斜地冲向他,撞飞了摩托车,撞碎了他的腿。刚刚23岁的他似乎到了生命的终点。

查德在痛苦中度过了7个月。躺在病床上,呆呆地看着穿过腿部连接骨头的钢针。一些骨头碎片已经丢在了马路上,一次次的手术也没能挽回截肢的命运。朋友们为他的手术组织了献血活动,上司为他保留着工作,希望他能回去继续工作。

当医生宣布要截肢后,查德陷入深深的绝望中。只剩下一条腿,还怎么工作?会让女人们厌烦吗?能结婚吗?能拥有自己梦想的家吗?能否支付起现在已经上升到三居室房价的高昂医药费?

截肢手术前,必须没有炎症。在等待期间,我们尽一切可能都无法让查德高兴起来或者减轻消沉的情绪。做这样的手术,如果查德根本不在乎死活,可不好办。

一天夜里,我带了同事的丈夫吉恩去查德的病房。一见面,吉恩就和查德聊了起来,和他开玩笑,说他是"一条腿已踏进了坟墓",说他"只能单腿独立了"。

查德愤怒了,厉声质问道:"他们就要切掉我的腿了,你怎么能来到我的房间说这样的话呢?"

吉恩只是不置可否地耸耸肩。然后弯下身去,松开了自己的假腿,扔到了查德的床上。我留下他们俩走了出来。

When I returned an hour later,Gene was gone and the light had come back into Chad's green eyes.

"You should hear his story! " Chad said."He stopped late at night on the freeway to change a flat tire.He was opening the trunk to fetch the spare when a drunk driver going sixty-five miles an hour honed in on his taillights and rear-ended Gene's car. Gene jumped as high as he could at the last moment,but one of his legs was cut clean off at the knee and the other was so badly mangled he came very close to losing it,too.The drunk driver had no insurance,and Gene had a wife and three children to support. And I thought I had problems! Gene manages the San Diego sports arena and is going to get me front-row tickets to my favorite rock band as soon as I recover from surgery and have learned to walk on a prosthesis! "His eyes softened then. "Gene says that people who give to others always get back more than they give.He said not to worry about my future.It will work out. He said the main thing was never to give up."

Four months later,Chad was back at work.He was selfconscious about his limp,exhausted at the end of every day,and the new prosthesis rubbed endless blisters on his tender stump. But he remembered Gene's words.He learned to ride a bicycle with his "fake leg", rode a horse bareback for the very first time,took off the prosthesis and swam one-legged in the ocean and at night when no one could see,he practiced running slow,jagged laps at the high school track.

A month after returning to work,Chad plucked up his courage and asked a pretty new girl at work if she'd like to go out with him.He was surprised when she said yes.He didn't know it then,but he had just asked out his future wife and mother of his three children-to-be.Jane didn't care how many legs Chad had.She cared only that he had a big heart.

一个小时后我回来时,吉恩走了,查德的碧眼重新现出了光彩。

"你该听听他的故事!"查德激动地说。"一天深夜,他在高速公路上停车换轮胎,正打开后背箱取备胎的时候,一个醉酒驾车的司机以每小时65英里的速度开车,没注意到尾灯,与吉恩的车追尾了。最后时刻,吉恩尽力向高蹦起来,可是一条腿仍被齐刷刷地撞没了,另一条腿也是血肉模糊,几乎没了。醉酒的司机没有任何保险。吉恩要养活妻子和3个孩子。我以为只有我才有这样的问题呢!吉恩管理圣迭戈体育场,只要我从手术中恢复过来,可以学会用假肢走路,他就送我前排票,看最喜欢的摇滚乐队演出。"他的眼睛变得温柔起来。"吉恩说给予他人的人获得的东西要比给予的多。不要担心未来,总会有办法的。重要的事情是永不放弃。"

4个月后,查德重新上班了。残疾让他很不舒服,每天工作结束时都疲惫不堪,新安的假肢在柔嫩的残腿根部磨出了很多水疱。但他记着吉恩说过的话。学习用假腿骑车,第1次在光光的马背上骑马,取下假肢单腿在海里游泳,夜深人静时,在学校凸凹不平的跑道上慢跑。

回到工作岗位一个月后,查德鼓起勇气问一个女同事是否愿意和他约会。当她说可以时,查德惊讶极了。他当时还不知道,这个他约会的女孩后来成为了自己的妻子和3个孩子的母亲。珍妮不在乎查德有多少条腿,只在乎他有颗宽广的心。

The hardest problem for Chad was wondering how he would ever get back on his "foot" financially.The hospital bills he owed would take thirty years to pay.He would never be able to afford a car or a home,but he refused to give up.He remembered Gene's words and paid whatever he could afford to the hospital twice a month.

Not long after he met Jane,one of his doctors called.Often they called to ask Chad to rush to the hospital and offer comfort and support to an injury victim facing amputation.No matter how tired or sore Chad was,no matter what hour of the day or night he was called,he never refused to drop everything and help out a fellow human being in need.But this call was different.

"Chad,"the doctor began, "because you underwent experimental procedures during the months we tried to save your leg,many people became acquainted with your case.I am calling to tell you that an anonymous stranger has just paid all your medical bills."

Gene was right.People who give freely to others get back more than they give.

Anita Grimm

CHICKEN SOUP

对查德而言,最难的事情是如何在经济上"立足"。医院的账单要花30年才能付清,他永远买不起汽车和房子,但他决不言弃。他记得吉恩说过的话,每月一次支付医院的账单。

在他遇到珍妮后不久,医生打电话来。通常他们打电话是让他快赶到医院劝慰面临截肢的病人。无论多么劳累,多么疼痛,无论是白天还是黑夜,只要接到电话,他从未拒绝,从未放弃去帮助需要的人们渡过难关。但这次电话不同。

"查德,"医生开口说,"为了挽救你的腿,这几个月中你做了不少尝试性的手术,很多人了解了你的情况。现在我打电话就想告诉你,一个不愿留姓名的陌生人刚刚支付了你所有的费用。"

吉恩说得对:无私奉献的人获得的要比给予的多。

安妮塔·克里姆

The Rose with No Thorns

Kindness is a language the dumb can speak and the deaf can hear and understand.

Christian Nestell Bovee

A young man carrying a guitar case boarded the afternoon school bus at Maple Street.Obviously ill at ease,he found a seat,placed the guitar on end beside him in the aisle,and held it upright with his arm.He looked around anxiously,then hung his head and began shuffling his feet back and forth on the floor of the bus.

Melanie watched him.She didn't know who he was,but from his looks she decided he must be a real loser.

Melanie's friend Kathy looked up from her book. "Wouldn't you know it?Crazy Carl again."

"Who's Crazy Carl?"Melanie asked,tossing her sunny hair.

"Don't you know your next-door neighbor?"

"Next-door neighbor?The Bells moved into that house.We met them the day we left on spring vacation."

"Well,that's his name,Carl Bell."

The bus rolled on under the big trees along Elm Street.Kathy and Melanie stared at the newcomer and his big guitar case.

When the driver called out "Sycamore",the new boy awkwardly picked up his case and got off.It was Melanie's stop,too,but she didn't budge.When the bus started again,she rang for the next corner. "See you, Kathy."

无刺玫瑰

友善是一种语言,失语者说得出,失聪者听得懂。

克里斯汀·内斯特尔·博韦

在枫叶街,一个年轻人携带着一个吉他箱子登上了下午的校车。显然,他感到有些不适应,找到座位后,把吉他竖在旁边的过道上,用胳臂支着它,然后紧张地四下环顾,垂下了头,双脚在校车的地上来回摩挲。

梅拉妮不认识这个人,但从他的外表看,一定是个不走运的人。

梅拉妮的朋友凯茜从书上抬起头说:"认识不?又是那个疯子卡尔。"

"谁是疯子卡尔?"梅拉妮甩动着金黄色的秀发问道。

"你不认识隔壁邻居?""隔壁邻居?贝尔家住进了隔壁,过春假出门时跟他们碰过面。"

"对,那就是他的名字,卡尔·贝尔。"

校车在榆树街高大的榆树下行驶,凯茜和梅拉妮盯盯地看着这个新乘客和他的大吉他。

司机喊出"悬铃木站"时,这个新上车的男青年笨拙地拿起吉他箱下了车。梅拉妮也在这站下车,但她没有动。车子重新启动,她按铃在下一个街角下了车。"再见,凯茜。"

Melanie ran home,up the steps and through the front door.She called out,"Mom,does that weirdo live next door?"

Her mother came into the hall from the kitchen."Melanie,you must not refer to anyone as a weirdo.Yes,the Bells have a handicapped son. This morning I called Mrs.Bell,and she told me about Carl.He has never been able to speak.He has a congenital heart defect and a nervous disorder.They have found a private tutor for him,and he is taking guitar lessons to help improve his coordination."

"Just the pits! Right next door! "Melanie exclaimed.

"He's a shy boy.You must be neighborly.Just say hello when you see him."

"But he rides the school bus,and the kids laugh at him."

"See that you don't,"her mother advised.

It was a week before Carl boarded the bus again.Melanie thought he recognized her.Grudgingly,she said hello.Some of the other kids started whispering and making jokes.Pretty soon spit wads were flying. "Settle down! "the driver yelled.Carl shuffled his feet.Each time a spit wad hit him he twitched.When his guitar clattered to the floor,the driver again admonished them to settle down—this time with a warning tone in his voice.The bus grew quiet but the fun didn't stop.The boys seated behind Carl started blowing on the back of his head,making his hair stand up.They thought is was funny.

When Sycamore Street came into view Carl jumped up,rang the bell,put the guitar strap over his shoulder and headed for the door.The guitar case swung wide,hitting Chuck Wilson on the neck.Carl rushed toward the door with his case still crosswise in the aisle.When Chuck caught up and took a swing at him,the shoulder strap tore loose and the case slid down the steps into the gutter.Carl stumbled off the bus and ran down the street,leaving his guitar behind.

Melanie sat glued to her seat."I'm never getting off there again,"

CHICKEN SOUP

梅拉妮一路跑回家，迈上台阶，穿过前门，大叫道："妈妈，那个怪物住在隔壁吗？"

妈妈从厨房来到了厅里，"梅拉妮，你不能把任何人叫做怪物。是的，贝尔家有个残疾儿子。今天早上，我给贝尔太太打电话，她告诉了我卡尔的事情，卡尔不会说话，患有先天性心脏病和神经错乱。他们给他找了一个私人教师上吉他课，帮助他改善协调性。"

"真倒霉！就住在隔壁！"梅拉妮抱怨道。

"卡尔很腼腆，你必须对他友善，见到他时向他问好。"

"但他乘校车时，男孩们都嘲笑他。"

"你可不能那么做。"妈妈提醒道。

一周后，卡尔又坐上了校车。梅拉妮以为他认出了她，满不情愿地向他打招呼。一些男孩开始窃窃私语，开起了玩笑。不久，口水就到处飞溅。"安静点！"司机大叫道。卡尔紧张地摩挲着双脚。每次口水吐到他，他的脸就抽动一下。当吉他撞到地上发出声响，司机就会又一次训斥男孩们让他们安静——这次声音里有了警告的语气。车子里安静下来，但玩笑并没有结束。坐在卡尔后面的男孩开始吹卡尔后面的头发，让头发竖起来。他们认为这很有趣。

悬铃木大街进入视线，卡尔跳了起来，按响了下车铃，然后把吉他挎在肩上，走向门口。吉他左右晃动得很厉害，碰到了查克·威尔逊的脖子。卡尔就快跑向门，吉他箱仍十字交错横在过道。查克追了上来，推了他一下，卡尔肩上的背带脱落了，吉他箱滑下车阶，掉进了排水沟。卡尔跟跄地下了车，跑向街道，丢下了他的吉他箱。

梅拉妮一动不动地坐着。"我再也不会在这儿下车了。"她对凯

she said to Kathy.Once again she waited until the next corner before getting off,then retraced the block back to Sycamore.The open case still lay in the gutter.She walked past it and headed toward home.*What a character!*she thought.*What did I ever do to deserve him for a neighbor?*

But by the time Melanie had gone half a block,her conscience bothered her for leaving Carl's guitar where anyone could pick it up.She turned back to get it.Both the handle and the strap on the case were broken,so she had to carry it in her arms with her books.*Why am I doing this?*she wondered.Then she remembered how terrible it had been when everybody laughed at him.

Mrs.Bell opened the door before Melanie could knock. "Melanie,I am so glad to see you! What happened?Carl was so upset he went straight to his room,"she said,laying the case on a chair.

"It was just a little accident."Melanie didn't want to alarm her with the whole story."Carl left his guitar.I thought I should bring it."

Carl didn't ride the bus after that.His parents drove him to and from guitar lessons.Melanie saw him only when he worked in his rose garden.

Life should have gone more smoothly,but kids still pestered him. They hung around his yard,threw acorns at him and chanted, "Crazy Carl,the banjo king,takes music lessons and can't play a thing."

One hot day as Carl relaxed on the grass with a soft drink,the kids came and started their chant.Melanie glanced out her window just in time to see the soda bottle shatter on the sidewalk at their feet.

The next day at school Kathy said,"Did you hear about Crazy Carl cutting those kids with a broken bottle?"

"No wonder,"Melanie said,"the way they keep after him."

"Whose side are you on?"Kathy fired back.

"I'm not choosing sides,but I heard them bugging him."

"Bet you two hold hands over the fence,"Kathy said sarcastically.

茜说,于是又一次坐到下一个街角才下车,然后沿着楼群回到了悬铃木大街。散开了的吉他箱仍然躺在排水沟里,她跨了过去,一直朝家走去。真是怪人!她想。我做了什么,怎么会成为他的邻居?

但是,走了半个街区的时候,一想到卡尔的吉他就扔在那里,任何人都可以拣到,她就感到心里隐隐不安。她转了回去,拣起了吉他。提手和肩带都坏了,她得抱着吉他和书本走。我为什么这么做?她困惑地想。接着,想起来大家嘲笑卡尔时令人不快的情形。

还没等梅拉妮敲门,贝尔太太就打开了门。"梅拉妮,真高兴见到你!发生了什么事?卡尔情绪低落,径自回到了自己的房间。"她说着,把吉他箱放在了椅子上。

"一次小意外,"梅拉妮不想告诉她,让她担心。"卡尔落下了吉他,我想该给他带来。"

从那以后,卡尔再没坐过校车,都是父母接送他上吉他课。只有在玫瑰园里干活时,梅拉妮才能看见他。

生活本可以风平浪静,可是男孩们仍然骚扰他,他们游荡在园子的周围,朝他扔果子,唱道:"疯子卡尔,乐器之王,学习吉他,干弹不响。"

炎热的一天,卡尔正悠闲地躺在草地上喝着汽水,那群男孩又来了,唱了起来。梅拉妮从窗户向外看去,正好看见汽水瓶在男孩们脚下的人行道上爆裂。

第2天,在学校里,凯茜说:"你听说疯子卡尔用破玻璃瓶弄伤了那些男孩们吗?"

"毫不奇怪,"梅拉妮说,"他们自找的。"

"你站在哪一边?"凯茜反驳道。

"这不是站在哪一边的事情,我听见他们一直在骚扰卡尔。"

"我敢打赌你们一定隔着篱笆握手了。"凯茜讽刺道。

At noon in the cafeteria line a classmate teased Melanie, "If you're asking Crazy Carl to go with you to the banquet, I'll be glad to take Jim off your hands."

Before the day was over, somebody wrote on the blackboard, "Melanie loves Crazy Carl."

Melanie managed to keep her poise just long enough to get home. She ran in the door and burst into tears. "Mom, I told you it was the pits having a weirdo next door. I hate him." She told her mother what happened at school.

"It hurts when your friends turn on you," Melanie said, "and for nothing! " Then she thought of something she hadn't considered before. "Carl must have cried lots of times."

"I'm sure," her mother agreed.

Why do I feel so mean about Carl? She wondered. *Or maybe I don't. Maybe I just think I'm supposed to because everybody else does.*

"Sometimes, Mom, I don't bother to do my own thinking." Melanie wiped her eyes. "Jim's coming over. I have to wash my hair." She ran upstairs.

On the last day of school, Melanie came home early. Carl was in his rose garden. When he saw her, he clipped a rose and went to the gate to wait. Melanie greeted him with her usual hello. He held out the rose. As she reached for it, he put up his other hand to delay her, and started breaking off the thorns. He pricked his finger, frowned a moment, wiped the blood on his shirt sleeve, and continued breaking off the thorns.

Tonight was the banquet, and Melanie wanted to get home and be sure her clothes were ready. But she stood and waited.

Carl handed her the rose with no thorns. "Thank you, Carl. Now I won't stick my fingers," she said, in an effort to interpret his thoughts. Touched by his childlike grin, she patted his cheek, thanked him again and walked on home. At the door she looked back. Carl was still standing

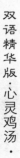

CHICKEN SOUP

双语精华版·心灵鸡汤·

中午在咖啡厅排队时，一位同学取笑梅拉妮说："如果你邀请疯子卡尔参加毕业晚宴，我就乐意把吉姆从你手中抢走。"

放学前，有人在黑板上写道："梅拉妮爱疯子卡尔。"

梅拉妮努力保持镇静，一回到家里，就跑进家，眼泪刷刷地淌。"妈妈，我说过，有一个怪物做邻居真倒霉，我恨他。"她告诉了妈妈发生在学校的事情。

"当朋友跟你过不去时，可真不好受，"梅拉妮说，"而且还是因为无中生有的事情跟你过不去。"她突然想起了以前从未想到的事情，"卡尔一定因此哭过很多次了。"

"肯定是。"妈妈赞同地说。

我为什么把卡尔想得这么低劣？她迷惑不解。也许没有这么想，也许只是认为应该这么想，因为其他人都这样。

"有时，妈妈，本不必自寻烦恼的。"梅拉妮擦干了眼泪说："吉姆要来了，我得洗下头发。"她跑上了楼梯。

学期的最后一天，梅拉妮早早回到了家。卡尔在花园里，当卡尔看见了她，就剪了一枝玫瑰，走到门口等她。梅拉妮像以前一样向他问候，卡尔伸出了玫瑰给她，她正要去接，卡尔却阻止了她，而是开始折断玫瑰上的刺。玫瑰刺刺伤了他的手，他皱了下眉，把血迹在衬衣袖子上擦了一下，接着折刺。

今天晚上就是毕业晚宴，梅拉妮想回家看看她的衣服是否准备停当，但是她却仍站在那里，等着卡尔。

卡尔递给了她无刺的玫瑰。"谢谢你，卡尔，现在就不会扎着手了。"她说着，努力去理解他心中的想法。被卡尔孩子般的笑容感动，她拍了拍他的脸颊，又一次感谢了他，然后走回家。在门口，回头望

there,holding his hand against the cheek she had touched.

One week later Carl died of congestive heart failure.After the funeral,the Bells went away for a while.

One day a letter came from Mrs.Bell.There was a special note for Melanie.

> *Dear Melanie,*
>
> *I think Carl would have liked you to have this last page from his diary.We encouraged him to write at least one sentence a day.Most days there was little good to write.*
>
> *Mr.Bell and I want to thank you for being his friend— the only youthful friend he ever had.*
>
> *Our love,*
> *Carla Bell*

Carl's last words:Melanie is rose with no thorns.

Eva Harding

CHICKEN SOUP

去,卡尔仍然站在那里,抚摩她拍过的脸颊。

一周之后,卡尔死于充血性心力衰竭。葬礼后,贝尔一家离家在外呆了一段时间。

一天,贝尔太太寄来了一封信,里面有专门写给梅拉妮的一个便条。

> 亲爱的梅拉妮:
>
> 我想卡尔希望你收到他日记的最后一页。他生前,我们鼓励他每天写一句话。大部分日子里,他几乎没有什么高兴的事情可写。
>
> 贝尔先生和我都想谢谢你成为他的朋友——他一生中唯一的年轻的朋友。
>
> 爱你的,
>
> 卡拉·贝尔

卡尔写的最后的话是:梅拉妮是无刺玫瑰。

伊娃·哈丁

Big Ed

When I arrived in the city to present a seminar on Tough-Minded Management, a small group of people took me to dinner to brief me on the people I would talk to the next day.

The obvious leader of the group was Big Ed, a large burly man with a deep rumbling voice. At dinner he informed me that he was a troubleshooter for a huge international organization. His job was to go into certain divisions or subsidiaries to terminate the employment of the executive in charge.

"Joe," he said, "I'm really looking forward to tomorrow because all of the guys need to listen to a tough guy like you. They're gonna find out that my style is the right one." He grinned and winked.

I smiled. I knew the next day was going to be different from what he was anticipating.

The next day he sat impassively all through the seminar and left at the end without saying anything to me.

Three years later I returned to that city to present another management seminar to approximately the same group. Big Ed was there again. At about ten o'clock he suddenly stood up and asked loudly, "Joe, can I say something to these people?"

I grinned and said, "Sure. When anybody is as big as you are, Ed, he can say anything he wants."

Big Ed went on to say, "All of you guys know me and some of you know what's happened to me. I want to share it, however, with all of you. Joe, I think you'll appreciate it by the time I've finished.

CHICKEN SOUP

大艾迪

有一次，我到这个城市参加一个有关强势性管理的研讨会，当地的人邀请我去赴晚宴，同时向我介绍第2天听我发言的对象。

很显然，这群人的头儿是大艾迪。他身材魁伟，声音洪亮。宴会中，大艾迪告诉我，他是一个跨国公司的斡旋人，他的工作就是到公司的各部门或者下属公司结束主管的工作。

"乔，"他说，"我非常盼望明天的到来，因为所有的人都需要倾听一下像你这样强硬派的讲话，这样他们就会明白我的风格正确无比。"他咧开嘴笑了，又向我眨眨眼睛。

我也笑了，因为我知道第2天会与他预想的完全不同。

第2天，研讨会从始至终，大艾迪都面无表情，一言不发，走时也没有和我打声招呼。

3年以后，我又回到这个城市，几乎对同一群观众做另一个有关管理的发言。大艾迪正好又出席了。大约10点钟时，他突然站了起来，大声地问："乔，我能跟大家说几句话吗？"

我笑道："当然。当人们到你这样的年龄，艾迪，想说什么都行。"

大艾迪说道："所有的人都认识我，有些人还知道我的经历。然而，我还是想给大家讲一下。乔，我想等我讲完时，你会感激我的。"

"When I heard you suggest that each of us,in order to become real-ly tough-minded,needed to learn to tell those closest to us that we really loved them,I thought it was a bunch of sentimental garbage.I wondered what in the world that had to do with being tough.You had said tough-ness is like leather,and hardness is like granite,that the tough mind is open,resilient,disciplined and tenacious.But I couldn't see what love had to do with it.

CHICKEN
SOUP

"That night,as I sat across the living room from my wife,your words were still bugging me.What kind of courage would it take to tell my wife I loved her?Couldn't anybody do it?You had also said this should be in the daylight and not in the bedroom.I found myself clearing my throat and starting and then stopping.My wife looked up and asked me what I had said,and I answered,'Oh nothing.'Then suddenly,I got up,walked across the room,nervously pushed her newspaper aside and said,'Alice,I love you.'For a minute she looked startled.Then the tears came to her eyes and she said softly,'Ed,I love you,too,but this is the first time in 25 years you've said it like that.'

"We talked a while about how love,if there's enough of it,can dis-solve all kinds of tensions,and suddenly I decided on the spur of the mo-ment to call my oldest son in New York.We have never really commu-nicated well.When I got him on the phone,I blurted out,'Son,you're li-able to think I'm drunk,but I'm not.I just thought I'd call you and tell you I love you.'

"There was a pause at his end and then I heard him say quietly, 'Dad,I guess I've known, that,but it's sure good to hear.I want you to know I love you,too.'We had a good chat and then I called my youngest son in San Francisco.We had been closer.I told him the same thing and this,too,led to a real fine talk like we'd never really had.

双
语
精
华
版
·
心
灵
鸡
汤
·

"上次，当我听到你建议说要想真正成为强硬派，就需要向身边最亲近的人表达真挚的爱意，我认为这是一套煽情的废话，这跟意志坚强有什么关系呢。你说过坚强的意志如同皮革，冷酷无情如同花岗岩，坚强的意志是开放式的，有弹性，有约束力，有韧性，但我还是不理解这跟爱有什么关系。"

"那天晚上，面对妻子坐在客厅里，你的话一直在我心中萦绕，告诉她我爱她需要多大的勇气？每个人都能做到吗？你还讲过，说我爱你这番话的时候要选白天，而不是在卧室里。于是，我清了清嗓子，刚想说，就停了下来。妻子抬起头，看见我欲言又止的样子，问我有话要说么，我答道：'哦，没什么。'突然，我站起来走过去，紧张地拿开她手中的报纸说道：'爱丽丝，我爱你。'她惊愕了一下之后，眼泪涌了上来，温柔地说：'艾迪，我也爱你。这是25年来你第1次说这话。'"

"我们聊了起来，说到如果有足够的爱，就可以消融所有的紧张关系。激动之下，我决定给我远在纽约的大儿子打个电话，我们从未很好地沟通过。电话打通了，我脱口而出：'儿子，你以为我喝多了，但是我没有，我只是想给你打电话告诉你我爱你。'"

"一阵沉默后，我听见他轻轻地说：'爸爸，我想我知道你爱我，可是能亲耳听你这么说，真是太好了。我也想让你知道，我也爱你。'我们开心地聊了一会儿，我又给在旧金山的小儿子打了电话，我们的关系一直比较亲密。我也告诉了他我爱他，于是就有了一次真正美妙的谈话。"

21

"As I lay in bed that night thinking,I realized that all the things you'd talked about that day—real management nuts and bolts—took on extra meaning,and I could get a handle on how to apply them if I really understood and practiced tough-minded love.

"I began to read books on the subject.Sure enough,Joe,a lot of great people had a lot to say,and I began to realize the enormous practicality of applied love in my life,both at home and at work."

"As some of you guys here know,I really changed the way I work with people.I began to listen more and to really hear.I learned what it was like to try to get to know people's strengths rather than dwelling on their weaknesses.I began to discover the real pleasure of helping build their confidence.Maybe the most important thing of all was that I really began to understand that an excellent way to show love and respect for people was to expect them to use their strengths to meet objectives we had worked out together.

"Joe,this is my way of saying thanks.Incidentally,talk about practical! I'm now executive vice-president of the company and they call me a pivotal leader.Okay, you guys, now listen to this guy! "

Joe Batten

"那天晚上躺在床上，我思绪万千，想到你那天讲到的所有关于真正管理方法的点点滴滴，豁然开朗。我要是真正理解了它们，就可以恰当地使用它们，实践真正强硬派的爱。"

"我开始阅读相关的书籍。的确，乔，很多大人物都有很多话要说，而我也开始意识到生活中爱的巨大作用，无论是在家里还是工作中。"

"正如你们所知，我改变了与人相处的方法。开始注重倾听，明白了如何了解别人的长处，而不是对他们的缺点抓住不放，开始找到了帮助他人建立信心的真正乐趣。也许最重要的事情是，我开始真正地明白表现爱和尊重最完美的方式是，相信人们可以利用自己的优势实现预定的目标。"

"乔，这就是我的感谢之处。顺便说一句，做事要讲究实效！我现在是公司的执行副总裁，人们称我为领导中枢。好了，伙计们，现在听这家伙讲话吧！"

乔·巴腾

A Treasure in Time

They that love beyond the world cannot be separated by it.Death cannot kill what never dies.

William Penn

CHICKEN SOUP

Interstate 40 stretched endlessly before me.I was coming home from the first family reunion without Bob,held in June of 1995.Memories of our short nine years of marriage flooded through me.

We both worked for the Social Security Administration and three years previously accepted positions in a field office in Oklahoma City,a transfer we needed for any future advancements.In February 1995,a 10-week training session for a promotion sent me to Dallas,Texas;a session cut short by the news of a bomb ripping through the Alfred P. Murrah Building in Oklahoma City.

My Bob was in that building.

When Bob and I first met,he was putting together a tape of love songs titled "20 years of Loving You," gleaned from albums and 45s borrowed from friends,some of whom were unattached women with their own agenda.I offered him the use of my record collection and asked him to use my favorite,Stevie Wonder's "I Just Called to Say I Love You."

By the time Bob finished the tape,we had been dating for several weeks.One Saturday,he called and said he had a surprise for me.As I got in the car and we headed for the highway,he took out a cassette and slid his finished tape into the tape deck.My own voice,taken from a message I once left on his answering machine,came out of the speaker: "I just

及时到来的珍宝

> 超凡脱俗的爱，是不可能被分离的，死亡也不能击败永恒。

威廉·佩恩

1995年的6月，是鲍博离开后我第1次单独去参加家庭聚会。现在我正行驶在回家的路上，前面是40号州际公路延伸的路面，脑海中不断涌出婚后短短九年的各种记忆。

我们两人都在社会安全管理局工作，3年前接受了俄克拉荷马市地方政府的一个新职位，换工作主要是为了将来的升职机会。1995年的2月，我去得克萨斯的达拉斯市参加一项10周的升职培训，培训没有结束就传来了阿尔佛雷德·P.莫拉大厦发生爆炸的消息。我的鲍博当时就在那幢楼里。

我和鲍博初次相遇时，他已在组合一盘情歌磁带，题目叫做《爱你20年》，收集各种歌曲录音集，也向朋友借各种45年的歌集，有些是那些独立的女性自己的歌集。我把自己录制的歌曲集交给他用，让他使用我最爱的那首歌，史蒂夫·旺德演唱的《电话诉衷肠》。

鲍博做完这盘磁带前几个星期，我们开始约会。一个星期六，他打电话给我，说要给我一个惊喜。当我们开车上了高速公路，他拿出一盘录音带，放入车上的放音机内，我自己的声音从扬声器中传了出来，"打电话告诉你……"声音是我曾经留在他的录音电话里的，

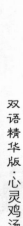

called…"The tape then faded into the music of Stevie Wonder."This one is especially for you," he said.

The memory brought tears to my eyes.Now,close to the Oklahoma state line,I happened to see the sign "Oklahoma Trading Post—50 Miles Ahead—Exit 287."　It occurred to me that Bob and I always meant to stop on our return trips from his family reunions in Florida,but we never did.We had already gassed up an exit or two before,We ere tired,we just wanted to get home."This time," I decided,"I'm going to stop."

As I drove,my mind wandered;how could I ever make it without Bob—my big,strong husband whose comforting arms held me when I cried,whose sense of humor melted my anger,and whose sense of adventure enriched both our lives.Tears stained my cheeks,but I kept driving. Suddenly,there was exit 287. Damn! I had passed the Trading Post.Well, maybe next time.

Just as suddenly as I made the decision to drive on,I decided I would go back! I swerved the car at the last instant and drove up the ramp.Reaching the main road,I realized I was on the Turner Turnpike— no exits for who knew how many miles.I looked for a flat place in the median and drove across,mindless of whether a state trooper might be watching,and headed back toward the Trading Post.

As expected,the Trading Post was like many Bob and I stopped at on our travels:a mixture of Southwestern goods and souvenirs.As I wandered through the store,I came upon a wrought-iron and wooden bed setup showcasing Indian blankets,prickly cactus plants and strings of red and green peppers.

Beside the bed was a small table holding Aztec vases,delicate desert flowers and a howling coyote with a bright scarf around its neck. Unobtrusively nestled among them sat a small,old-timely wooden telephone with a carved mouthpiece and rotary dial,its receiver resting on the black prong and connected with a thin black cord.My first

双语精华版·心灵鸡汤·

声音渐渐淡化在史蒂夫·旺德的音乐中。他说："这是我特别为你制作的。"

回忆让我泪眼朦胧，现在车离俄克拉荷马州很近了。我无意中看到路标上写着："俄克拉荷马服务站——前方50公里——287出口。"我突然想起，以前我和鲍博到佛罗里达与他家人团聚，回来的路上常想在那儿停一下，但一直都没有停。因为已经在前面的出口处加过油。我们太累了，想回家了。而这一次，我决定要停一下。

一边开车，我的脑子一边在想，没有了鲍博我该怎么办，我的高大强壮的丈夫，在我哭的时候，总是用他那温暖的双臂拥着我，用他的幽默融化我的怒气，用他的探索精神丰富我们的生活，眼泪顺着我的脸颊流淌下来，我继续开着车，突然看见287出口。天哪！我错过了服务站。那么，下次再去吧。

我刚刚想要开过去，又突然决定要转回头，在最后一刻。猛地转向把车开向斜道进入主道时，我想如果进了调头区，前方不知还有多少路才有出口，我看见中间地带的一片平地，就横穿过去，也不顾是否有骑马的巡警看见，一直向服务区开去。

正如我预期的那样，服务区就像我和鲍博以前旅行时见到的许多服务区一样，里面陈列着来自西南部的商品和纪念品，我在店中漫步，看到那些铁制或木制的陈列架，陈列着印度的毛毯，多刺的仙人掌，穿成串的红绿椒等。

架子边有个小桌子，放着阿芝台克的花瓶，精致的花，还有一只带着一条鲜艳领巾的狼狗。在这些东西中间，不起眼地安置着一架老式的木制电话，话筒上有刻花，老式的拨号盘。一条黑色的细线连

thought was, "How unusual.Everything else is so Southwestern,the telephone looks out of place." Picking it up,I lifted the receiver.

A musical tinkling began from the base of the phone.Tears filled my eyes and coursed down my cheeks.A wave of warmth swept over me as I stood sobbing,clutching the phone,oblivious of other customers walking warily around me.The tune I heard was "I Just Called to Say I Love You."

Making my way toward the front to pay for my newly-found treasure,there was no doubt now that I could make it.I was not alone;my Bob had just called to say he loved me.

Judy Walker

着放在黑色叉架上的听筒。我的第一反应是:"多么奇特,这里的所有东西都是西南部风格的,而这部电话显得很不相称。"我拿起话筒举向耳边。

清脆的音乐声从电话里响起,眼泪立刻涌满眼眶,顺腮边流下来,一股暖流传遍全身,我站在那儿紧紧握着电话哭泣着,忘了周围还有其他顾客,电话听筒中传出的音乐是《电话诉衷肠》。

我走到出口处付钱买下了新发现的珍宝,毫无疑问,我要这么做,我不是孤单的,我的鲍博打电话告诉我他爱我。

茱迪·沃克

THE FAMILY CIRCUS. By Bil Keane

10-29
©1996 Bil Keane, Inc.
Dist. by Cowles Synd., Inc.

经典系列／光阴的故事

"I'm a real superhero. I'm Daddy."

My Dream House and My Boy

CHICKEN SOUP

There must be more to life than having everything.

Maurice Sendak

It seemed the perfect place to raise a family:a beautiful lot in Spokane,Washington,surrounded by ponderosa pines,near forests and streams.When my wife,Joy,and I found it,we knew it was the ideal site for our dream house.

The lot was expensive,far beyond what I could afford on my modest salary as a philosophy professor at Whitworth College. But I started teaching extra classes and moonlighting in real estate.

We finally bought the lot.Sometimes I'd put my infant son,Soren,in a backpack and take him for walks in our future neighborhood. "You'll love roaming these fields and streams," I'd tell him.

Then came the wonderful summer when I helped the contractor build our home.My brother-in-law,a California architect,had designed elaborate plans as a gift. I'd work sunup to sundown,rush home for dinner and often go teach a night class. Confronted with choices for materials,I'd always answer, "Give us the best.We're going to be here for a lifetime."

I'd take one of our girls,Sydney,five,or Whitney,seven,with me whenever I had errands to run.But at the dinner table,I'd just nod as the girls tried to tell me about their day.Rarely was my mind fully with our family.Instead,I'd be worrying about the escalating costs of the house.

理想之屋与儿子

生活中一定有比拥有所有东西都重要的事情。

莫里斯·桑达克

　　这里似乎是安家的理想之所：这片美丽的宅地位于华盛顿的斯波肯，依山傍水，四周环绕着北美黄松。妻子乔伊和我发现它时，就断定这就是我们梦寐以求的房子。

　　这块宅地很昂贵，远远超出我在惠特沃斯学院当哲学教授所挣的微薄薪水。于是，我开始在外授课，还在房地产业兼职。

　　终于买下了这块宅地。有时，我用背包背着褓襁中的儿子索林到未来的家周围转转。"你一定会喜欢在这田野和溪水中玩耍的。"我对他说。

　　美妙的夏天来了，我们协助承包商建了自己的家。妹夫是位加利弗尼亚的建筑师，精心设计了效果图，作为礼物送给了我们。我每天一大早就开始干活，一直干到日头下山。然后急忙忙赶回家吃饭，再去夜校上课。在选择何种建筑材料时，我的回答总是"选最好的，我们要在这住一辈子呢。"

　　实在忙不开时，就把5岁的女儿希德尼和7岁的儿子惠特尼带上。在餐桌上，当孩子们告诉我一天的事情时，只是点头应付。心思很难放在家里，而是一直牵挂着不断增加的房子的花销。

But we made it—a four-year goal fulfilled! I felt pride and satisfaction the day we moved in.I loved helping my children explore the neighborhood to meet new friends.

Only a week later,we had to move out.

Unable to sell our other home,we'd arranged to rent it to meet the house payments.At the last minute,the renters backed out."We can make it somehow," I assured Joy.But she faced the truth of our overextended finances,"Forrest,we wouldn't own the house;it would own us."

Deep down,I knew she was right.The exquisite setting and distinctive architecture meant our new home would sell faster than the old.I reluctantly agreed,but disappointment led to lingering depression.

One afternoon,I drove to the new house just to think.To my surprise,I was engulfed with a sense of failure and started to cry.

That fall and winter,I kept wondering why this loss bothered me so much.My studies in religion and philosophy should have taught me what really matters—it's what I try to help my students understand.Still,my mood remained bleak.

In April,we all went on vacation to California with Joy's parents. One day we took a bus trip to the Mission of San Juan Capistrano,where swallows return each March from Argentina.

"Can I feed the pigeons?" begged Whitney,heading toward the low, stone fountain inside a flower-filled courtyard.The four adults took turns taking kids to feed the birds,visit the souvenir shop and enjoy the manicured grounds.When it was time to get back to the bus,I looked for Joy and found her with the girls and their grandparents.

"Where's Soren?" I asked.

"I thought he was with you."

A horrible fear hit as we realized it had been nearly twenty minutes

我们终于成功了,4年的目标实现了！搬家的那天,我感到骄傲和满足。我喜欢带着孩子们四处转转,交交朋友。

可仅仅一周后,我们就不得不搬了出去。

因为不能卖掉另一处房子,我们决定把它租出去用来支付房屋的费用。可是,租房子的人最后时刻打了退堂鼓。"我们一定能租出去的,"我宽慰乔伊说。面对透支的财政状况,她说:"福雷斯特,我们成不了房子的主人,而它却成了我们的主人。"

内心深处,我知道她说得对。新房子,环境典雅,建筑设计独特,一定比老房子好卖。我不情愿地同意了。但失望让我消沉了很长时间。

一天下午,我开车来到新房子,想好好思考一下。让我吃惊的是,失败带来的挫败感吞没了我,我哭了。

那年的秋天和冬天,我一直在思考,为什么这次失落让我这么痛苦。我学习宗教和哲学,它们应该教会我什么是重要的东西,这也是我帮助学生理解的事情。然而,我的思想还是一片空白。

4月,我们和乔伊的父母一起到加利弗尼亚度假。一天,我们乘大巴车来到燕子教堂游玩。每年3月,燕子都会从阿根廷返回到燕子教堂。

"我可以喂鸽子吗？"惠特尼恳求道,走向满是鲜花的庭院中一个低矮的石头喷泉。4个大人轮流带孩子喂鸽子,逛纪念品商店,享受着修剪整齐的草地。该回车上了,我寻找乔伊,看见她正和女孩子们和外公、外婆在一起。

"索林在哪儿？"我问道。

"我以为他和你在一起。"

一阵可怕的恐惧袭来,我们意识到已经有20分钟没有见到索林

since anyone had seen him.Soren was a very active twenty-two-month-old who loved to explore.Fearless and friendly,he could be anywhere by now.

We all started running through the five acres of the mission grounds."Have you seen a little red-haired boy this high?" I asked everyone I saw.I ran into back gardens,behind buildings,into shops.No Soren.I started to panic.

Suddenly I heard Joy scream "No! " Then I saw Soren,lying on the edge of the fountain,arms outstretched.He was blue,bloated and looked lifeless.The sight burned like a branding iron in my mind.It was one of those moments when you know deep inside that life will never be the same.

A woman cradled Soren's head as she gave him mouth-to-mouth resuscitation,and a man pressed on his chest."Is he going to be all right?" I yelled,fearing the truth.

"We're doing the right things," the woman said.Joy collapsed on the ground,saying over and over,"This can't be happening."

*Lord,don't let him die,*I prayed.But I knew he couldn't be alive,not after nearly twenty minutes underwater.

In less than a minute,paramedics arrived,connected Soren to life-support systems and rushed him to the hospital.A trauma team pounced on him,led by a specialist in "near drownings".

"How's he doing?" I kept asking.

"He's alive," said one of the nurses,"but barely.The next twenty-four hours are critical.We want to helicopter him to the Western Medical Center in Santa Ana." She looked at me with kindness and added, "Even if he lives,you must realize there's a strong chance of significant brain damage."

了。索林才22个月大，非常活泼，对人友好，喜欢探险，胆子特大，现在说不定在哪儿呢。

在5英亩的教堂四周，我们四处奔跑，寻找着他。"你看见过一个这么高、红头发的小男孩了吗？"我问见到的每一个人。跑进后园、楼后、商店寻找着。没有索林。我开始感到恐慌。

突然，我听到乔伊的尖叫声"不"。然后看见了索林，躺在喷泉的边上，胳臂伸展着。他脸色铁青，浑身浮肿，像是没了气息。这情景像铁烙一样在脑海中留下印记，让人刻骨铭心，我知道生活将永远不一样了。

一位妇女搂着索林，给他做人工呼吸，一位男士正按着索林的胸部。"他会有事吗？"我叫道，害怕这变成事实。

"我们正做该做的事情。"妇女说。乔伊瘫倒在地上，一遍又一遍地呢喃："这不可能！"

上帝呀，不要让他死，我祈祷着。但我知道他可能活不了了，尤其是在溺水近20分钟后。

不到一分钟，救护人员就赶到了，给索林上了呼吸机，飞快地送他到医院。由一位"溺水"专家领头的紧急救援小组立即实施抢救。

"他怎么样了？"我不断地问。

"他活着，"一位护士说，"但仍有危险。接下来的24小时非常关键。我们想用直升机送他到桑特安娜的西部医疗中心。"她友善地看着我，又补充道："即使活下来，你必须知道严重脑部损伤的几率非常大。"

Nothing could have prepared me for the sight of my young son in the intensive care unit at Western.His limp,naked body was dwarfed by the machines connected to him by countless wires.A neurosurgeon had bolted an intracranial pressure probe into his head between the skull and the brain.The bolt,screwed into the top of his head,had a wing nut on top.A glowing red light was attached to his finger.He looked like E.T.

Soren made it through the first twenty-four hours.For the next forty-eight hours,we stayed by his side while his fever skyrocketed past 105 degrees.We sang his favorite bedtime songs,hoping we could soothe his hurt even in his comatose state.

"You both need to take a break," insisted our doctor.So Joy and I went for a drive and started to talk.

"There's something besides Soren that's really bothering me," I told her."I've heard that when couples go through a tragedy like this,it may separate them.I couldn't bear to lose you,too."

"No matter what happens," she said,"this isn't going to break us up.Our love for Soren grew out of our love for each other."

I needed to hear that,and then we started to cry,laugh and reminisce,telling each other what we loved about our mischievous son.He delighted in balls,and before he was even a year old I'd hung a miniature basketball hoop in his bedroom. "Remember how he scooted in his walker and tried to land one,squealing 'yeaaa' if he came near?" I asked.

We also discussed our fears about brain damage."The doctor seems more hopeful now," I reminded Joy.He had told us Soren was alive only because all the right things were done immediately after he was found. Thinking earlier that we'd lost him,we felt grateful he even had a fighting chance.We'd take him any way we could get him.But we wondered what the impact would be on the family if brain damage was extensive.

CHICKEN SOUP

儿子躺在急救病房的情景是我无法预料到的。他光裸、软弱的身体与连接在他身上、插着无数电线的机器比起来,是那么渺小。神经外科医生把一个颅内压探针固定到索林的颅骨和脑组织之间。这根上端带蝶形螺母的螺栓探针钻进了他的头顶。一个发光的红灯接在他的手指上。他看起来像个外星人。

索林成功地度过了24小时。接下来的48小时,大家坐在他的床边。他的体温一路攀升,高达105度。我们唱着他在床上爱听的歌曲,希望抚慰他的伤痛,即使在他昏迷的状态中。

"你们俩需要休息。"医生坚持道。我和乔伊就出来兜风,聊了起来。

"除了索林,还有一件事让我担心,"我告诉她,"听说,夫妻经历这样的悲剧时,很可能会分手。我不能忍受失去你的痛苦。"

"无论发生什么事,"她安慰道,"都不会让我们分开。对索林的爱来自我们之间的爱。"

我需要听到这样的话。我们开始哭着、笑着、回忆着淘气的儿子可爱之处。他喜欢球,没到1岁,我就给他在卧室里挂了一个小型篮筐。"记得他在学步车里快走的样子吗?总想进一个球,球一接近篮筐就尖叫'呀'。"

我们也谈到了对脑部损伤的恐惧。"医生现在更有信心了。"我提醒乔伊。医生告诉我,索林活着,就是因为在他被发现之后,所有该做的事情都及时地做了。以前想到会失去他,现在还有搏斗的机会,我们都已经很感激了。无论如何,我们不能失去他。同时也想到了如果大范围脑部受损,会对家庭带来的影响。

"Can you believe that,for these past months,what mattered to me was losing that house?" I asked. "What good would a new house be if we came home to an empty bedroom?"

Even though Soren was still unconscious,that conversation gave us some peace.We'd also been receiving wonderful support from friends, family and strangers and felt the power of their prayers.

In the following days,four visitors dropped by to see Soren.First came Dave Cameron,who had discovered Soren underwater.A Vietnam veteran,he led tours at the mission. "I arrived early that morning.Standing near the fountain,I suddenly had this strong sense of foreboding,"he said. "That's when I saw the backs of his tiny tennis shoes.Instinct and training took over from there."

Soon after came Mikiel Hertzler,the woman who applied mouth-to-mouth resuscitation until the ambulance arrived. "I've been trained in CPR," she told us. "When I first saw him,I couldn't find a pulse.But faint bubbles in the back of his throat made me think he was trying to breathe."

I shuddered.*What if someone with less medical knowledge had discovered him and given up sooner?*

Then two strapping paramedics,Brian Stephens and Thor Swanson, told us that they were usually stationed ten minutes away,but that day they were on an errand a block from the mission when they got the call.

As we remembered the doctor's words about Soren's being alive only because all the right things happened immediately,their stories touched us deeply.

On the third night,the phone woke me in the hospital room my wife and I were using. "Come quick," shouted Joy. "Soren's waking up! " When I got there,he was slowly stirring,rubbing his eyes.In a few hours, he regained consciousness. But would he ever be the same boy who had brought such exuberance to our home?

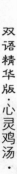

"过去的几个月中，相信吗，我所一直牵挂的是失去那所新房子，"我说，"如果回家看到卧室空空的，新房子又好到哪里呢？"

索林还未苏醒，但这次谈话让我们都平静下来。我们一直得到了家里人、朋友和陌生人的支持，感受到了他们祈祷的力量。

在接下来的几天里，4位客人来看索林。首先来的是戴夫·卡梅伦，他发现了水下的索林。他是位越南退伍兵，带领布道团四处传教。"我今天早上到的。站在喷泉边，突然有一种强烈的不祥的预感，"他说，"那是我看到他的小网球鞋的时候。本能和多年的训练帮了我的忙。"

不久，米基艾尔·赫茨勒来了，在救护车来之前，就是她对索林进行的人工呼吸。"我一直接受心肺修复术的训练，"她告诉我们，"开始时，找不到脉搏。但是他喉咙后面微小的气泡让我想到，他正努力呼吸。"

我一阵寒栗。如果发现他的人没有多少医学知识，提前放弃抢救呢？

然后是身材魁伟的救护员布莱恩·斯蒂芬斯和索尔·斯旺森。他们告诉我们，通常他们呆在离事发地点10分钟远的地方，那天正好到距离一个楼群的地方办事，一听到呼叫，马上赶来了。

我们想起医生的话，索林之所以活着，就是因为所有该做的事情都及时做了。这些客人讲的故事深深地感动了我。

第3天晚上，在医院给我和妻子安排的房间里休息。电话铃惊醒了我。"快回来，"乔伊大声叫道，"索林醒了！"到医院时，索林正缓慢地、轻轻地动着，揉搓着眼睛。几小时后，他恢复了意识。但他还仍然是那个给全家带来生机的男孩吗？

A couple of days later,Joy was holding Soren in her lap.I had a ball in my hand.He tried to get it—and he said,"Ball." I couldn't believe it! Then he pointed to a soda.I brought it to him with a straw,and he started to blow bubbles.He laughed—a weak,feeble laugh,but it was our Soren! We laughed and cried;the doctors and nurses did,too.

Just a few weeks later,Soren was racing around our home,bouncing balls and chattering as usual.Full of rambunctious energy,he gave us all a sense of wonder at the gift of life.

Almost losing Soren helped me look closely at my role as a father. What really matters is not that I provide my children the ideal house,the perfect playroom,even woods and rivers.They need me.

Recently,I drove back to my dream home.Prisms of sunlight shone through its fifty-two windows and,yes,it has a beautiful site.But I wasn't troubled anymore,and I know why.As I returned home to take the kids on a promised picnic,all three ran out.Soren squealed, "Daddy,Daddy, Daddy! " And I had time to play.

Forest Baird

As told to Linda Lawrence

几天后，乔伊把索林抱到大腿上，我手里握着球。索林要抓球，说道："球。"我简直不能相信！然后，他指向汽水。我把带吸管的汽水给他，他开始吹泡泡。他笑了，一种微弱的、无力的笑，可这就是我们的索林！大家喜极而泣。医生和护士们也留下了欢喜的泪水。

仅仅几周后，索林就能在房子周围撒欢儿了，像以往一样边拍球边唧唧喳喳地说话。他浑身充满了朝气和活力，让我们感受到生命的奇迹。

索林有惊无险的经历帮我认真审视做父亲的角色。真正重要的不是给孩子们提供理想的房子、完美的游戏室，甚至森林和河流。他们需要的是我这个人。

最近，我开车回到了那个梦想的房子。52个窗户间透射出菱形的阳光。是的，这是一个美丽的住宅。但我不再为之烦恼，我知道原因所在。我回到家里，履行诺言，带孩子们去野餐。3个孩子跑出来，索林尖叫道："爸爸，爸爸，爸爸！"我与孩子们同乐。

福雷斯特·贝尔德

（琳达·劳伦斯整理）

经典系列／光阴的故事

Crying's Okay

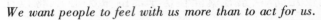

We want people to feel with us more than to act for us.

George Eliot

CHICKEN SOUP

My parents made me go to school that day even though I felt as if I couldn't stand to be around anyone.Where can you get away from people in a schoolhouse?

Finally I wandered into the room where I have English because no one was there except Mrs.Markle,and she was busy grading papers.I sat down across the desk from her.She just looked up at me and smiled as if there was nothing strange about a kid coming to the English room when he didn't have to.

"He's dead,"I said in a strangled voice.

"John?"

I nodded."He was my best friend."

"Yes,I know,Kirk."She walked over and closed the door,then came back to her desk.

"I miss him,"I said.

"I know,"she said again, "and that hurts.When something really hurts,it's all right to cry."She put a box of tissue in front of me and went on grading papers while I broke down and bawled.I was relieved that she didn't look at me.

"Nothing like this ever happened to me before,"I said. "I don't know how to handle it."

"You don't have much choice,"she told me. "John is gone and he won't be back."

想哭就哭

我们想让人们分享感受，而不仅仅为我们做事。

乔治·艾略特

那天，尽管我觉得还是不能与人相处，但父亲强迫我上学。学校哪有避开人的地方呀？

最后我还是不情愿地挪到上英语的教室，因为那里只有马克尔夫人一个人，她正忙着改卷子。我坐到桌子的对面，她只是抬头看我笑了笑，就好像一个孩子走进了本不属于自己的英语教室一样，没有什么好奇怪的。

"他死了。"我哽咽着说。

"约翰？"

我点点头。"他是我最好的朋友。"

"是的，我知道，柯克。"她走过去，关上门，然后回到自己的桌旁。

"我想他。"我说。

"我知道，"她又说道，"这一定令人伤心。真正伤心的时候，就大哭一场吧。"她把一盒纸巾放在我面前，继续批改卷子。我伤心欲绝，大哭起来。她没盯着我，我感觉哭得很痛快。

"以前从未经历过这事，"我说，"我不知道该怎么办。"

"你没有多少选择，"她劝慰道，"约翰走了，不会再回来了。"

"But what do I do?"

"Just keep on hurting until you begin to heal a little."

"I don't think I'll ever get over his death."

"You will someday,even though right now you can't believe you ever will."

"I guess."

"That's because we know with our minds,"Mrs.Markle said, "but we believe with our feelings."

I sat and thought about that for a while.

"You might make things easier for John's family by visiting them," Mrs.Markle gently suggested.

I hadn't thought about John's family until now.If this was rough on me,what must it be for them?

"John's parents don't like me,"I explained. "They think I was bad news for John."

"And probably your folks weren't wild about your running around with John."

"That's right."I was surprised at how much Mrs.Markle seemed to know.Just a plain old English teacher.

"That's how it is with parents,"she said. "Young people together do things they wouldn't have the nerve to do by themselves.So parents get the idea that their sons and daughters are being led astray by their friends."

"Hey,that's about it."

"Go see John's family,Kirk.They'll change their minds about you now.You'll see.And if they don't,you will have at least given it a try."

"I feel guilty about some of the things John and I did,"I said. "Maybe God makes us feel guilty to punish us."

Mrs. Markle shook her head."I don't think God plans for us to carry big loads of guilt along through life.He does give us a conscience,

"可我怎么办？"

"一直伤心下去，直到伤口愈合。"

"我想，我无法从他的死亡中解脱出来。"

"终有一天，你会的，尽管你现在认为你不能。"

"但愿吧。"

"那是因为人们用头脑获得认知，"马克尔夫人说，"但却要用情感获得信任。"

我坐在那里，琢磨着她说的话。

"去看望一下约翰的家人，你就不会这么痛苦了。"马克尔夫人温柔地建议。

这之前，我从未想到过约翰家人。如果约翰的死对我都残酷，对他的家人呢？

"约翰的家人不喜欢我，"我解释道。"他们认为我是丧门星。"

"很可能你家人对你和约翰一起乱跑却不怎么大惊小怪。"

"对呀。"我很惊讶，马克尔夫人似乎知道一切。

"父母都是这样，"她说，"年轻人做父母没勇气做的事情，父母就认为他们的孩子被朋友带坏了。"

"嘿，就是这么回事。"

"去看看约翰的家人，柯克。他们会改变对你的看法的。你会看到的。如果他们不改变想法，你至少努力了。"

"我为约翰和我做过的一些事情感到内疚，"我说，"也许上帝就想让我们内疚作为一种惩罚。"

马克尔夫人摇了摇头。"我认为，上帝没打算让我们背着沉重的负担度过一生。但他确实给了我们良心，这样我们可以乞求宽恕，从

though,so we can ask forgiveness,and so we can profit from our mis-takes.That's how we grow into better human beings."

That seemed to make good sense,but I didn't know how to quit feeling guilty.Mrs.Markle seemed to know what I was thinking.She said, "Guilt can be a crutch,you know."

"A crutch?"

"Yes,indeed.Guilt is a sort of self-punishment.If you feel guilty enough,you don't have to do something about yourself."

"'Something about yourself'?"

"Like improving your behavior,for instance."

The first bell rang.I stood up to go.

"By the way,"Mrs.Markle said,"I'm glad you weren't with John in that car when it crashed."

"That's something else I feel guilty about,"I admitted."About John getting killed and not me."

Mrs.Markle said, "That's one thing you should not feel guilty about—being alive when someone else dies."

"Oh,"I said. "Well,thanks for helping me.My folks didn't under-stand how I felt."

"How do you know?"

"They made me come to school."

"Perhaps that's because they did understand.They probably figured you'd be better off at school with classmates to share your grief."

"Oh.I didn't think about that.I wonder…"

The thought of going to see John's family was the hardest thing I can remember having to do.I wanted to talk to my parents about it,but I was afraid they wouldn't understand.Still,Mrs.Markle had said they might be more understanding than I realized.

At dinnertime Mom said, "We know you feel bad about John.Is there anything you'd like to talk about?"

双语精华版·心灵鸡汤·

错误中受益。我们人类就会变得更好。"

她的话很有道理，但我还是不知道怎样不再内疚。马克尔夫人似乎看出了我的心思，说道："知道吗，内疚也是支柱。"

"支柱？"

"是的，实实在在的支柱。内疚是一种自我惩罚。惩罚足够时，就不再对自己苛求了。"

"苛求？"

"比如说，改进你的行为。"

头一遍铃响了，我站起身要走。

"另外，"马克尔夫人说，"我很高兴，车出事时，你没和约翰在一起。"

"这也是我感到内疚的事情，"我坦白地说。"约翰出事死了，而我没有。"

马克尔夫人说："别人死了，而你活下来，这没有什么可内疚的。"

"噢，"我说，"好吧，谢谢你开导我。家里人可不理解我的感受。"

"你怎么知道？"

"他们强迫我上学。"

"也许那是因为他们太理解你的感受了。很可能他们认为有同学和你一起分享悲伤，你会好点。"

"哦，这我可没有想过。我想知道……"

想到去见约翰的家人，是我最头疼的事情。想跟父母商量，可担心他们不理解。但是，马克尔夫人说过，他们也许比我认为的要开明得多。

晚餐时，妈妈说："我们知道你为约翰难过。你有什么话想说吗？"

That gave me the opening I needed."I ought to go see John's fami-ly,but they probably don't want to see me."

"Why not?"Dad asked.

"On account of how John and I got into trouble sometimes."

"Sorrow sometimes brings people closer together,"my mother said. "If I were John's parent,I'm sure I'd appreciate your coming."

So I forced my legs to take me to John's house.A lady I didn't know opened the door and took me to the living room.John's mother,fa-ther and sister sat there like broken dolls,staring into space.I didn't know what to do,but I tried to imagine they were my parents instead of John's.Then it seemed natural to go over and put my arm across Mrs. Roper's shoulder.When I did that,she began to cry.She put her arm around my waist and her head against my shoulder. "Forgive me for breaking down,"she said."I thought I was all cried out."

"It's all right to cry,"I told her.And all of a sudden I was crying, too.John's sister,Adele,was only eleven,but she came over then and put her arms around her mother and me.I began to feel sorry for John's dad, sitting there all by himself.After a little while I went over to him and put my hand on his arm.

"I'm glad to hear you say it's all right to cry,"he told me. "I keep wanting to do that."

Some other people came into the room about that time,so I said I guessed I'd better go.

Mrs. Roper walked to the door with me. "Kirk,it was so comforting to see you."

"I was afraid you didn't like me too much,"I said.

"We love you because John loved you.And Kirk,don't fret about the past.You and John weren't perfect;you were just acting like teenage boys,that's all.It's no one's fault John is dead."

"I'll come again,"I promised.

这就给我一个开口的机会。"我应该去看看约翰的家人,但他们很可能不想见我。"

"为什么不想?"爸爸问。

"因为我和约翰爱惹麻烦。"

"悲伤有时把人们拉得更近,"妈妈说,"如果我是约翰的父母,看见你来,一定会很感激的。"

我强挪双腿来到约翰的家。一位陌生的女士开门把我领进客厅。约翰的母亲、父亲和妹妹坐在那里,像伤心的木偶目光呆滞。我不知道如何是好,努力把他们想象成自己父母,而不是约翰的父母。很自然地走过去,拥抱了罗普尔夫人的肩膀。拥抱时,她开始哭泣。她的双手抱着我的腰部,头枕在我的肩膀上。"对不起,我实在控制不住,"她呜咽地说,"我想我的心都碎了。"

"想哭就哭吧。"我劝慰她。我也情不自禁地哭了起来。约翰的妹妹阿黛拉只有12岁,走过来,搂住她妈妈和我。约翰的爸爸一直孤独地坐在那里,我感觉有些冷落了他。过了一会儿,我走过去,手放在他的臂上。

"听到你说,想哭就哭吧,我很高兴,"他告诉我,"我一直就想哭。"

这时,其他人走进房间,我说我该走了。

罗普尔夫人送我到门口。"柯克,见到你我很欣慰。"

"我还担心你不喜欢我呢,"我说。

"我们爱你,因为约翰爱你。柯克,不要为过去的事情烦恼了。你和约翰不完美,你们只是做了青年人常做的事情,仅此而已。约翰的死不是任何人的错。"

"我会再来的。"我许诺道。

"Oh, Kirk, will you? It would mean so much to us."

I walked home feeling better than I had since that end-of-the-world minute when I heard that my best friend was dead. Tomorrow I would tell Mrs. Markle about the visit to John's family.

Kirk Hill

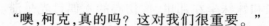

"噢,柯克,真的吗？这对我们很重要。"

听到最好的朋友约翰的死讯,就像世界末日的到来。走在回家的路上,我却感到了从未有过的轻松。明天,我将告诉马克尔夫人我去看望约翰家人的事情。

柯克·希尔

"And how do you feel about *that* perspective?"

Fourteen Steps

Adversity introduces a man to himself.

Anonymous

They say a cat has nine lives,and I am inclined to think that possible since I am now living my third life and I'm not even a cat.

My first life began on a clear,cold day in November,1904,when I arrived as the sixth of eight children of a farming family.My father died when I was 15,and we had a hard struggle to make a living.Mother stayed home and cooked the potatoes and beans and cornbread and greens,while the rest of us worked for whatever we could get—a small amount at best.

As the children grew up,they married,leaving only one sister and myself to support and care for Mother,who became paralyzed in her last years and died while still in her 60s.My sister married soon after,and I followed her example within the year.

This was when I began to enjoy my first life.I was very happy,in excellent health,and quite a good athlete.My wife and I became the parents of two lovely girls.I had a good job in San Jose and a beautiful home up the peninsula in San Carlos.

Life was a pleasant dream.

Then the dream ended and became one of those horrible nightmares that cause you to wake in a cold sweat in the middle of the night.I became afflicted with a slowly progressive disease of the motor nerves, affecting first my right arm and leg,and then my other side.

双
语
精
华
版
·
心
灵
鸡
汤
·

十四级台阶

逆境助你成人。

佚名

人们说猫有9条命,我相信那是可能的,因为我还不是猫,我现在已经有第3次生命了。

我的第1次生命诞生于1904年11月一个晴朗而又寒冷的日子,是这个家庭8个孩子中的第6个。我15岁时,父亲去世了,我们生活很艰难,妈妈在家里为我们煮土豆、菜豆、玉米及蔬菜等,而其他人必须为我们吃的、那很少的一点东西辛苦工作。

孩子们渐渐长大离开了,家里只剩下一个姐姐和我支持照顾着妈妈。妈妈在她生命的最后一年瘫痪了,去世时60多岁。之后,姐姐很快出嫁了,同年我也如她那样结了婚。

从这时开始,我的第1次生命散发着光彩,我非常幸福,非常健康,是一名非常棒的运动员。我和妻子有两个可爱的女儿。在圣何塞市有很好的工作,在圣·卡洛斯半岛有美丽的家。

生命宛如美妙的梦境。

然而,美梦结束了。跟着而来的可怕的噩梦让你半夜一身冷汗地惊醒。慢性渐进性运动神经疾病让我非常痛苦,它开始影响我的右臂和右腿,接着是身体的其他部分。

Thus began my second life...

In spite of my disease I still drove to and from work each day,with the aid of special equipment installed in my car.And I managed to keep my health and optimism,to a degree,because of 14 steps.

Crazy?Not at all.

Our home was a split-level affair with 14 steps leading up from the garage to the kitchen door.Those steps were a gauge of life.They were my yardstick,my challenge to continue living.I felt that if the day arrived when I was unable to lift one foot up one step and then drag the other painfully after it—repeating the process 14 times until,utterly spent,I would be through—I could then admit defeat and lie down and die.

So I kept on working,kept on climbing those steps.And time passed. The girls went to college and were happily married,and my wife and I were alone in our beautiful home with the 14 steps.

You might think that here walked a man of courage and strength. Not so.Here hobbled a bitterly disillusioned cripple,a man who held on to his sanity and his wife and his home and his job because of 14 miserable steps leading up to the back door from his garage.

As I dragged one foot after another up those steps—slowly,painfully,often stopping to rest—I would sometimes let my thoughts wander back to the years when I was playing ball,golfing,working out at the gym,hiking,swimming,running,jumping.And now I could barely manage to climb feebly up a set of steps.

As I became older,I became more disillusioned and frustrated.I'm sure that my wife and friends had some unhappy times when I chose to expound to them my philosophy of life.I believed that in this whole world I alone had been chosen to suffer.I had carried my cross now for nine years and probably would bear it for as long as I could climb those 14 steps.

这时,我的第2次生命开始了。

尽管有病我每天还是借助车上安装的专用设施开车上下班。更进一步的是因为有14级台阶,我努力保持我的健康和乐观。你认为我说疯话吗?一点也不是。

我住的房子是错层建筑,从车库进入厨房的门有14级台阶。这些台阶是我衡量生命的标准,是我挑战生命的准绳。我认为,只要我还能抬起一只脚放到上一层台阶上,再强忍痛苦把另一只脚拖上来。竭尽全力重复这样的动作14次,哪怕筋疲力尽,我的生命将继续,否则,一切都完了,我就会认输、倒下来、死去。

所以我坚持工作,坚持爬台阶。随着时间一天天的过去,女儿们上了大学,幸福地结了婚。妻子和我被孤独地留在这栋有14级台阶的漂亮房子里。

你也许会想这是一个具有勇气和力量的人,但你错了,这儿行走着一个非常痛苦、步履蹒跚的跛子。因为有引导他从车库进入后门的悲惨的14级台阶,这跛子才可能保持他健全的心智,他的妻子,他的家,他的工作。

当我慢慢地沿台阶一级一级往上挪时,剧痛难忍,常不得不停下休息,此时,就会让头脑去回想辉煌的过去,回想我在打球,打高尔夫,在体育馆运动徒步旅行、游泳、跑步、跳跃等,只有这样才能继续往上爬。

年纪越来越大,我也更加清楚,更加沮丧,我肯定我的妻子和朋友们有时对我的生活哲学并不太满意。我确信整个世界只有我一个人选择这样承受痛苦,这个十字架我已经背负9年了,也许,只要我还能爬上那14级台阶,我将永远背负着它。

I chose to ignore the comforting words from 1 Cor.15:52:"In a moment,in the twinkling of an eye…we shall be changed." And so it was that I lived my first and second lives here on earth.

Then on a dark night in August,1971,I began my third life.I had no idea when I left home that morning that so dramatic a change was to occur.I knew only that it had been rougher than usual even getting *down* the steps that morning.I dreaded the thought of having to climb them when I arrived home.

It was raining when I started home that night;gusty winds and slashing rain beat down on the car as I drove slowly down one of the less-traveled roads.Suddenly the steering wheel jerked in my hands and the car swerved violently to the right.In the same instant I heard the dreaded bang of a blowout.I fought the car to a stop on the rain-slick shoulder of the road and sat there as the enormity of the situation swept over me.It was impossible for me to change that tire!Utterly impossible!

A thought that a passing motorist might stop was dismissed at once. Why should anyone?I knew I wouldn't! Then I remembered that a short distance up a little side road was a house.I started the engine and thumped slowly along,keeping well over on the shoulder until I came to the dirt road,where I turned in—thankfully.Lighted windows welcomed me to the house and I pulled into the driveway and honked the horn.

The door opened and a little girl stood there,peering at me.I rolled down the window and called out that I had a flat and needed someone to change it for me because I had a crutch and couldn't do it myself.

She went into the house and a moment later came out bundled in raincoat and hat,followed by a man who called a cheerful greeting.

I sat there comfortable and dry,and felt a bit sorry for the man and the little girl working so hard in the storm.Well,I would pay them for it. The rain seemed to be slackening a bit now,and I rolled down the window all the way to watch.It seemed to me that they were awfully slow

我不想使用那些令人鼓舞的语言,如在克尔,15:52中写的:"那一刻,在闪亮的眼神中,我们将要改变。"就这样,我度过了我在地球上的第1次和第2次生命。继而,1971年8月的一个漆黑的夜晚,我开始了我的第3次生命,我已经不记得那天早上我是什么时候离开家的,以至带来那戏剧化的改变。我只记得早上离开家时下台阶比平时更困难,我很恐惧地想到回家时还得爬上这些台阶。

　　那晚回家时天在下雨,风很大,淅沥的雨敲打着车子。我开着车慢慢地行驶在一条人烟稀少的路上, 突然我紧握着的方向盘失灵,车猛地拐向右边,同时听到恐怖的爆胎声。我努力将车停靠在被雨淋得滑滑的路边,坐在那儿一筹莫展。我是不可能自己去换胎的。绝对不可能的。

　　想着可能有路过的车,但是一辆也没有,我知道没办法了。我想起沿着一条小的岔路,不远处有座房子。我启动发动机,沿着路边慢慢前行,终于看到泥土路。谢天谢地,房屋窗户上的灯光欢迎着我。我开下车道,按响了喇叭。

　　门开了,一个小女孩站在那儿看着我,我摇下车窗,告诉她我的车胎爆了,需要人帮忙换胎,因为我是个跛子自己换不了。

　　她走进去,过了一会儿穿着雨衣帽冲出来,后面跟着一位男士,高高兴兴地跟我打招呼。

　　我浑身干干的,舒舒服服地坐在那儿,对在暴雨中辛苦换胎的男人和小女孩有一丝歉意。是的,我会付钱给他们,现在雨小了一点。我一直开着车窗往外看。觉得他们干得非常慢,渐渐地我开始失

経典系列／光阴的故事

and I was beginning to become impatient.I heard the clank of metal from the back of the car and the little girl's voice came clearly to me. "Here's the jack-handle,Grandpa." She was answered by the murmur of the man's lower voice and the slow tilting of the car as it was jacked up.

There followed a long interval of noises,jolts and low conversation from the back of the car,but finally it was done.I felt the car bump as the jack was removed,and I heard the slam of the trunk lid,and then they were standing at my car window.

He was an old man,stooped and frail-looking under his slicker.The little girl was about eight or 10,I judged,with a merry face and a wide smile as she looked up at me.

He said,"This is a bad night for car trouble,but you're all set now."

"Thanks," I said,"thanks.How much do I owe you?"

He shook his head. "Nothing.Cynthia told me you were a cripple— on crutches.Glad to be of help.I know you'd do the same for me.There's no charge,friend."

I held out a five-dollar bill."No! I like to pay my way."

He made no effort to take it and the little girl stepped closer to the window and said quietly,"Grandpa can't see it."

In the next few frozen seconds the shame and horror of that moment penetrated,and I was sick with an intensity I had never felt before.A blind man and a child! Fumbling,feeling with cold,wet fingers for bolts and tools in the dark—a darkness that for him would probably never end until death.

They changed a tire for me—changed it in the rain and wind,with me sitting in snug comfort in the car with my crutch.My handicap.I don't remember how long I sat there after they said good night and left me,but it was long enough for me to search deep within myself and find some disturbing traits.

去耐心,我听到车后部传来金属的叮当声,小女孩清晰的声音传来:"这是千斤顶的把手,爷爷!"她回答着男人低低的耳语般的问题。慢慢地车身开始倾斜,被顶了起来。接着从车后传来一阵噪声、摇晃和低低的对话声,终于完成了,我感到千斤顶移开,车触地了,听到车厢后盖砰地关上的声音,接着看到他们站在我的车窗边。穿着雨衣的他是个老人,弯腰屈背,看起来很衰弱。小女孩大约8至10岁,她抬头看着我,那是一张愉快的充满笑容的脸蛋。

男人说:"天太糟了,车这时出事真麻烦,不过现在全弄好了。"

"谢谢你,"我说,"我该付你多少钱?"

他摇摇头说:"不用付钱,欣思亚告诉我你是用拐杖的,很高兴能帮助你。我知道,你也会这样对我,我们是免收费用的朋友。"

我拿出一张5美元的纸币递给他说:"不,我要付。"

他没有一点接钱的反应。小女孩走近我的车窗悄悄告诉我:"爷爷看不见。"

接下来静静的几秒钟,羞愧及惊恐冲击着我,我受到从未有过的巨大刺激。一个盲人和一个孩子,在冷雨中,用湿湿的手指在一片黑暗中,对他来说可能是永久的一片黑暗中,摸索着那些螺钉和工具。

他们为我换了一个车胎,在风雨中为我换胎,而我抱着我的拐杖、我的障碍坐在温暖、舒服的车里。我不记得,他们和我道过晚安离开后,我在那儿坐了多久,但久得足以让我进行深深的反思并寻找症结。

I realized that I was filled to overflowing with self-pity,selfishness, indifference to the needs of others and thoughtlessness.

I sat there and said a prayer.In humility I prayed for strength,for a greater understanding,for keener awareness of my shortcomings and for faith to continue asking in daily prayer for spiritual help to overcome them.

I prayed for blessings upon the blind man and his granddaughter.Finally I drove away,shaken in mind,humbled in spirit.

"Therefore all things whatsoever ye would that men should do to you,do ye even so to them:for this is the law and the prophets." (Matt.7: 12.)

To me now,months later,this scriptural admonition is more than just a passage in the Bible.It is a way of life,one that I am trying to follow.It isn't always easy.Sometimes it is frustrating,sometimes expensive in both time and money,but the value is there.

I am trying now not only to climb 14 steps each day,but in my small way to help others.Someday,perhaps,I will change a tire for a blind man in a car—someone as blind as I had been.

Hal Manwaring

我意识到在我的思想中充满了自我怜悯、自私自利、从不关心其他人的需要，而且遇事欠考虑。

我坐在那儿祈祷。由于自责，我乞求上天赐予我力量。让我能大彻大悟，能了解自己的缺陷，能坚定信念每日祈祷，能得到改正缺点的精神帮助。

我祈祷上天眷顾那位盲人和他的孙女。最终思想受到震撼，精神无比沮丧地开车离开了。

"你想要别人帮你做任何事，那么，你至少也要同样对待他们。因为这是法律和神谕。"（摘自马特7:12）

现在，几个月过去了，圣经中的这句忠告对我来说不仅仅是摘自圣经的一句话。它是我的生活准绳，我努力的方向。虽然并不容易，时而遭到挫败，时而从时间和财力上花费巨大，但意义不同凡响。

我现在不仅每天坚持爬上14级台阶，还尽我微薄之力去帮助别人，或许有一天，我要帮一位坐在车里的盲人换轮胎，就像那盲人帮我那样。

哈尔·曼沃林

For Me To Be More Creative, I Am Waiting For...

CHICKEN SOUP

1. Inspiration
2. Permission
3. Reassurance
4. The coffee to be ready
5. My turn
6. Someone to smooth the way
7. The rest of the rules
8. Someone to change
9. Wider fairways
10. Revenge
11. The stakes to be lower
12. More time
13. A significant
    relationship to:
    (a) improve
    (b) terminate
    (c) happen
14. The right person
15. A disaster
16. Time to almost run out
17. An obvious scapegoat
18. The kids to leave home

19. A Dow-Jones of 1500
20. The Lion to lie down with the Lamb
21. Mutual consent
22. A better time
23. A more favorable horoscope
24. My youth to return
25. The two-minute warning
26. The legal profession to reform
27. Richard Nixon to be reelected
28. Age to grant me the right of eccentricity
29. Tomorrow
30. Jacks or better
31. My annual checkup
32. A better circle of friends
33. The stakes to be higher
34. The semester to start
35. My way to be clear
36. The cat to stop clawing the sofa
37. An absence of risk

为了更有创造力，
我正等待……

经典系列／光阴的故事

38. The barking dog next door to leave town

39. My uncle to come home from the service

40. Someone to discover me

41. More adequate safeguards

42. A lower capital gains rate

43. The statute of limitations to run out

CHICKEN SOUP

44. My parents to die (Joke!)

45. A cure for herpes/AIDS

46. The things that I do not understand or approve of to go away

47. Wars to end

48. My love to rekindle

49. Someone to be watching

50. A clearly written set of instructions

51. Better birth control

52. The ERA to pass

53. An end to poverty,injustice, cruelty,deceit, incompetence, pestilence, crime and offensive suggestions

54. A competing patent to expire

55. Chicken Little to return

56. My subordinates to mature

57. My ego to improve

58. The pot to boil

59. My new credit card

60. The piano tuner

61. This meeting to be over

62. My receivables to clear

63. The unemployment checks to run out

64. Spring

65. My suit to come back from the cleaners

66. My self-esteem to be restored

67. A signal from Heaven

68. The alimony payments to stop

69. The gems of brilliance buried within my first bumbling efforts to be recognized, applauded and substantially rewarded so that I can work on the second draft in comfort

70. A reinterpretation of *Robert's Rules of Order*

71. Various aches and pains to subside

72. Shorter lines at the bank

73. The wind to freshen

74. My children to be thoughtful, neat,obedient and self-supporting

75. Next season

76. Someone else to screw up

38. 邻家的吠狗远离城市

39. 叔叔退伍返乡

40. 伯乐

41. 更充分的保障

42. 更低的资本利得率

43. 限制性法规的失效

44. 父母去世(开玩笑！)

45. 疱疹或者艾滋病的药方

46. 不理解或不赞成的事情如
    烟消散

47. 战争结束

48. 重新点燃爱之火

49. 关注的人

50. 一清二楚的指示

51. 更好的生育控制

52. 平等权利修正案通过

53. 贫困、不公、残暴、欺骗、无
    能、瘟疫、犯罪和谗言消除

54. 与之竞争的专利到期

55. 忧天小鸡迷途知返

56. 下属成熟

57. 自我提高

58. 等待已久的水壶终于开了

59. 新的信用证

60. 钢琴调音师

61. 会议结束

62. 收回欠款

63. 失业补助花光

64. 春天

65. 西装从干洗处取回

66. 恢复自尊

67. 天堂传音

68. 不再交赡养费

69. 在跟跄初行中深藏的智慧光
    芒被感知、欢呼和奖赏,这样
    我就能从容自得地再次上路

70.《罗伯特议事规则》

71. 各种疼痛缓解

72. 银行排队的队伍变短

73. 风更清新

74. 孩子们善于思考,整洁干
    净,孝敬自立

75. 下一个季节

76. 对他人发号施令

77. My current life to be declared a dress rehearsal with some script changes permitted before opening night
78. Logic to prevail
79. The next time around
80. You to stand out of my light
81. My ship to come in
82. A better deodorant
83. My dissertation to be finished
84. A sharp pencil
85. The check to clear
86. My wife, film or boomerang to come back
87. My doctor's approval,my father's permission,my minister's blessing or my lawyer's okay

88. Morning
89. California to fall into the ocean
90. A less turbulent time
91. The Iceman to Cometh
92. An opportunity to call collect
93. A better write-off
94. My smoking urges to subside
95. The rates to go down
96. The rates to go up
97. The rates to stabilize
98. My grandfather's estate to be settled
99. Weekend rates
100. A cue card
101. You to go first

David B. Campbell

大卫·B. 坎贝尔

The Flower in Her Hair

She always wore a flower in her hair.Always.Mostly I thought it looked strange.A flower in midday?To work?To professional meetings? She was an aspiring graphic designer in the large,busy office where I worked.Every day she'd sail into the office with its ultra-modern crisp decor,wearing a flower in her shoulder-length hair.Usually color-coordinated with her otherwise suitable attire,it bloomed,a small parasol of vivid color,pinned to the large backdrop of dark brunette waves.There were times,like at the company Christmas party,where the flower added a touch of festivity and seemed appropriate.But to work,it just seemed out of place.Some of the more "professionally-minded" women in the office were practically indignant about it,and thought someone ought to take her aside and inform her of the "rules" in being "taken seriously" in the business world.Others among us,myself included,thought it just an odd quirk and privately referred to her as "flower power" or "girl flower."

"Has flower power completed the preliminary design on the Wal-Mart project?" one of us would ask the other,with a small lopsided smile.

"Of course.It turned out great—her work has really blossomed," might be the reply,housed in patronizing smiles of shared amusement. We thought our mockery innocent at the time.To my knowledge no one had questioned the young woman as to why a flower accompanied her to work each day.In fact,we probably would have been more inclined to question her had she shown up without it.

发间鲜花

　　她总是在发间戴朵花，一直戴着，我总是觉得很奇怪，大白天戴朵花？去上班？去开工作会议？她是一个热情洋溢的美术设计师，和我同在一家大型的兴旺的工作室工作，每天她去工作室上班，都是那样超现代的舞台装扮，在齐肩发上戴一朵花，通常依据不同服装的颜色调整花的颜色，一把色彩鲜艳的女用小阳伞衬着她微黑的皮肤一起飘动。有时候，如公司的圣诞晚会时，那朵花增添了节日气氛，就显得比较合适。但是，工作的时候就比较扎眼。公司那些较职业化的女员工实际上对此已很不满，认为应该有人把她叫到一边，告诉她在工作的地方必须端庄一点，这是规矩。另一些同事，包括我在内认为这不过是她的一时的怪癖，私下里叫她"花痴"或"花妞"。

　　有的同事带着一丝坏笑故意问："难道花痴也是一种原始的市场设计？"

　　"当然，这创意太伟大了，她的设计一流。"回答多半是这样。大家把施恩的笑意藏起来共同拿此取乐。我们觉得我们当时的嘲笑并无恶意。我记得没有人问过这位年青女士为什么每天戴朵花上班，事实上，我们经常会问她能不能不要戴花。

Which she did one day.When she delivered a project to my office,I queried."I noticed there is no flower in your hair today," I said casually. "I'm so used to seeing you wear one that it almost seems as if something is missing."

"Oh,yes," she replied quietly,in a rather somber tone.This was a departure from her usual bright and perky personality.The pregnant pause that followed blared loudly,prompting me to ask,"Are you okay?" Though I was hoping for a"Yes,I'm fine" response,intuitively,I knew I had treaded onto something bigger than a missing flower.

"Oh," she said softly,with an expression encumbered with recollection and sorrow."Today is the anniversary of my mother's death.I miss her so much.I guess I'm a bit blue."

"I understand," I said,feeling compassion for her but not wanting to wade into emotional waters."I'm sure it's very difficult for you to talk about," I continued,the business part of me hoping she would agree,but my heart understanding that there was more.

"No.It's okay,really.I know that I'm extraordinarily sensitive today. This is a day of mourning,I suppose.You see⋯"and she began to tell me the story.

"My mother knew that she was losing her life to cancer.Eventually, she died.I was 15 at the time.We were very close.She was so loving,so giving.Because she knew she was dying,she prerecorded a birthday message I was to watch every year on my birthday,from age 16 until I reached 25.Today is my 25th birthday,and this morning I watched the video she prepared for this day.I guess I'm still digesting it.And wishing she were alive."

"Well,my heart goes out to you," I said,feeling a great deal of empathy for her.

有一天，她没有戴花。她到我的办公室交设计稿时，我问："今天怎么没有戴花？"我顺嘴说："我已经习惯了你戴朵花，这样好像缺少了什么。"

"嗯，是的。"她平静地回答。声音很忧郁，和她平日欢快而张扬的个性完全不符。张扬变成沉默必有原因，所以我问："你还好吗？"虽然希望回答："是的，我很好。"但我的直觉告诉我一定有什么比没戴花更重大的事。"噢，"她轻轻说，带着回忆与悲伤的表情，"今天是我母亲去世周年纪念日，我太想她，有点难过。"

"我懂了。"我说，有点同情她但情绪没有受到太大的触动，"提到这些你一定觉得难吧。"我继续说，从一般交往上来说希望她赞成我的话，但我内心却感到她有更多的话要说。

"不，没关系，我知道我今天特别敏感，我想今天是悲伤的日子，不是吗？"接着她开始告诉我那些事。

"我母亲得了癌症，知道自己不久于人世。最后，她去世了，那时我只有15岁，我和妈妈非常亲密。她那么有爱心又那么为我付出，知道自己就要死了，事先录制了生日祝词让我在每年生日那一天观看。从16岁一直到25岁。今天是我25岁生日，早上我观看了她为今天准备的录像。我想，我还是感伤，希望她还活着。"

"是的，我也这样想。"我充满同情地对她说。

CHICKEN SOUP

"Thank you for your kindness," she said. "Oh, and about the missing flower you asked about. When I was a little girl, my mother would often put flowers in my hair. One day when she was in the hospital, I took her this beautiful large rose from her garden. As I held it up to her nose so she could smell it, she took it from me, and without saying a word, pulled me close to her, stroking my hair and brushing it from my face, placed it in my hair, just as she had done when I was little. She died later that day." Tears came to her eyes as she added, "I've just always worn a flower in my hair since—it made me feel as though she were with me, if only in spirit. But," she sighed, "today, as I watched the video designed for me on this birthday, in it she said she was sorry for not being able to be there for me as I grew up, that she hoped she had been a good parent, and that she would like a sign that I was becoming self-sufficient. That's the way my mother thought—the way she talked." She looked at me, smiling fondly at the memory. "She was so wise."

I nodded, agreeing. "Yes, she sounds very wise."

"So I thought, a sign, what could it be? And it seemed it was the flower that had to go. But I'll miss it, and what it represents."

Her hazel eyes gazed off in recollection as she continued. "I was so lucky to have had her." Her voice trailed off and she met my eyes again, then smiled sadly. "But I don't need to wear a flower to be reminded of these things. I really do know that. It was just an outward sign of my treasured memories—they're still there even with the flower gone…but still, I will miss it…Oh, here's the project. I hope it meets with your approval." She handed me the neatly prepared folder, signed, with a hand-drawn flower, her signature trademark, below her name.

When I was young, I remember hearing the phrase, "Never judge another person until you've walked a mile in his shoes." I thought about

"谢谢你的关心，"她说，"噢，刚才你问我为什么没有戴花，那是因为我很小的时候，妈妈经常在我头上戴朵花。而那天，我在医院里，我从她的花园里摘了一朵很大的美丽的玫瑰花带给她，当我把花举到她鼻子边让她闻香味时，她从我手中拿走花，一句话没说，把我拉过去，抚顺我的头发，花朵从我面前掠过，插在我的头上。就像我小时候她常常做的那样。那天的晚些时候，她就走了。"眼眶里含满了泪水，她接着说："从那时起，我就每天在发间戴朵花。这让我感觉她还和我在一起，哪怕只是精神上在一起。"她叹了口气："今天，当我观看她为这个生日录制的录像时，她在录像中说她很抱歉不能陪我长大。她希望自己是个好母亲，更希望能看到我已经长大能够自立的一个标记。那就是我妈妈所想的，所说的。"她边说边看着我，因回忆而略显天真地微笑着："她真聪明。"

我点点头说："是的，听起来真的很聪明。"

"所以，我想，一个标记，什么才能是这样的标记呢？好像是那朵花该离开的时候了。但是，如果不再戴花，可以吗？"

她回忆着，淡褐色的眼睛凝视着别处，继续说道："有这样的母亲，我很幸运。"她的声音慢慢变小。她再次看着我，悲伤地笑了笑："但是，我不再需要戴朵花来提醒我这些事情。这一点我明白，那只是我那些珍贵记忆的外表的标记。即使不戴花那些记忆也在。那么我将不再戴花了。哦，这是我的设计，希望你能认可。"她递给我准备好的整整齐齐的文件夹，签名的下面有一朵画上去的花朵作为她签名的标记。

我小的时候，听说过这样一句话："穿上他的鞋行走一英里后再

all the times I had been insensitive about this young woman with the flower in her hair, and how tragic it was that I had done this in the absence of information, not knowing the young woman's fate and the cross that was hers to bear. I prided myself on knowing intricately each facet of my company, and knew precisely how each role and function contributed to the next. How tragic for me that I had bought into the notion that a person's personal life was unrelated to her professional life, and was to be left at the door when entering corporate life. That day I knew that the flower this young woman wore in her hair was symbolic of her outpouring of love—a way for her to stay connected to the young mother she had lost when she herself was a young girl.

I looked over the project she had completed, and felt honored that it had been treated by one with such depth and capacity for *feeling* ... of *being*. No wonder her work was consistently excellent. She lived in her heart daily. And caused me to revisit mine.

Bettie B. Youngs
From Gifts of the Heart

去评价这个人。"我觉得一直以来,我对发间戴朵花的年轻女士缺乏了解,在不知实情的情况下我的那些表现真的很可悲。不知道那女士的命运及所背负的十字架,满足于从同事那儿七拼八凑得来的消息,错误地认为个人生活与职业生涯毫无关系,将之拒于集体之外。那一天,我知道了,那女人发间戴的花是她表示爱的象征,是她与自己很小时候就已过世的年轻妈妈联系的纽带。

我看了她完成的设计,感到非常钦佩,她是将深厚的情感及领悟融入其中精工细作的。怪不得,她的工作一贯非常出色,因她每日全心投入生活。这也让我重新审视我的人生。

贝蒂·B.杨
摘自《心灵的礼物》

You Don't Bring Me Flowers, Anymore

CHICKEN SOUP

Pain and suffering is inevitable, being miserable is optional.

Art Clanin

The elderly caretaker of a peaceful lonely cemetery received a check every month from a woman, an invalid in a hospital in a nearby city. The check was to buy fresh flowers for the grave of her son, who had been killed in an automobile accident a couple of years before.

One day a car drove into the cemetery and stopped in front of the caretaker's ivy-covered administration building. A man was driving the car. In the back seat sat an elderly lady, pale as death, her eyes half-closed.

"The lady is too ill to walk," the driver told the caretaker. "Would you mind coming with us to her son's grave—she has a favor to ask of you. You see, she is dying, and she has asked me, as an old family friend, to bring her out here for one last look at her son's grave."

"Is this Mrs. Wilson?" the caretaker asked.

The man nodded.

"Yes, I know who she is. She's the one who has been sending me a check every month to put flowers on her son's grave." The caretaker followed the man to the car and got in beside the woman. She was frail and obviously near death. But there was something else about her face, the caretaker noted—the eyes dark and sullen, hiding some deep,

请不要再给我送花来

悲痛和伤心是难免的，然而悲惨也是可选择的。

阿特·克莱宁

一个平静而又偏僻的公墓里年老的看墓人，每个月都会收到一位女性寄来的支票，这位女性是一个病人，住在邻近城市的一家医院里，她寄来支票是用来购买鲜花放在她儿子的坟墓上，她的儿子在几年前的车祸中去世了。

一天，一辆车开进公墓，停在常春藤覆盖着的管理楼前，一个男人开车，车后座坐着一名老年妇女，脸色苍白，半闭着眼睛。

开车的人告诉看墓人："这位女士病得快要死了，能麻烦你带我们去他儿子坟上吗——她有些事想请你帮忙。你瞧，她快要死了，我是她们家的老朋友，她要我带她来这儿最后看一眼她儿子的坟。"

"是威尔逊女士吗？"看墓人问。

那人点点头。

"是的，我知道她是谁了，她就是那位夫人，每月都寄一张支票给我，让我买花放在她儿子的墓上。"看墓人跟着他上了车坐在女士旁边。她很虚弱，看起来是快要死了。然而，看墓人注意到在她的脸上还有一些其他的东西，眼神忧伤而阴沉，隐藏着深深的、长久

long-lasting hurt.

"I am Mrs. Wilson," she whispered. "Every month for the past two years—"

"Yes, I know. I have attended to it, just as you asked."

"I have come here today," she went on, "because the doctors tell me I have only a few weeks left. I shall not be sorry to go. There is nothing left to live for. But before I die, I wanted to come here for one last look and to make arrangements with you to keep on placing the flowers on my son's grave."

She seemed exhausted—the effort to speak sapping her strength. The car made its way down a narrow, gravel road to the grave. When they reached the grave, the woman, with what appeared to be great effort, raised herself slightly and gazed out the window at her son's tombstone. There was no sound during the moments that followed —only the chirping of the birds in the tall, old trees scattered among the graves.

Finally, the caretaker spoke. "You know, Ma'am, I was always sorry you kept sending the money for the flowers."

The woman seemed at first not to hear. Then slowly she turned toward him. "Sorry?" she whispered. "Do you realize what you are saying—my son..."

"Yes, I know," he said gently. "But, you see, I belong to a church group that every week visits hospitals, asylums, prisons. There are live people in those places who need cheering up, and most of them love flowers—they can see them and smell them. That grave—" he said, "over there—there's no one living, no one to see and smell the beauty of the flowers..." he looked away, his voice trailing off.

The woman did not answer, but just kept staring at the grave of her son. After what seemed like hours, she lifted her hand and the man drove them back to the caretaker's building. He got out and without a word they drove off. *I've offended her,* he thought. *I shouldn't have said what I did.*

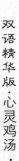

的悲痛。

"我是威尔逊夫人，"她低低地说，"两年来，每个月……"

"我知道，我都按你要求的那样做了。"

"今天，我到这儿来，"她接着说，"是因为医生告诉我，我只剩下几个星期了，死对我来说没有什么，活下来也没有什么意义了。但在我死前，我想最后到这儿来看一看，并要作好安排，请你继续在我儿子的坟上放花。"

她仿佛很疲惫，这番话耗尽了她的力气。车沿着墓道间窄窄的路向前开，到了她儿子墓前，女士好像用尽力气微微欠起身从车窗向外看着儿子的墓碑，此刻，周围一片寂静，只有散布在墓碑间老树上的鸟儿的鸣叫声。

终于，看墓人说："要知道，太太，你不断寄钱来买花，让我一直觉得很遗憾。"

女士起初好像没听见，后来慢慢转向他小声说："遗憾，为什么？你在说什么——我儿子……"

"是的，我知道，"他轻轻地说，"但是，你瞧，我是信教徒，每个星期都要去医院、救济院、监狱等处，那儿有许多活着的人需要鼓励，他们大部分人都喜爱花，他们能看到并闻到花香。那儿的那座坟里，已经没有活着的人了，没有人可以看到和闻到这些美丽的花……"他说着，把头转开，声音慢慢低下去。

女士什么也没说，眼睛一直盯着儿子的坟墓。仿佛过了几个小时，她抬起头，开车人把车开回管理处。看墓人下了车，他们一句话没说就开车走了。他想，我得罪她了，我不该说那些。

Some months later,however,he was astonished to have another visit from the woman.This time there was no driver.She was driving the car herself! The caretaker could hardly believe his eyes.

"You were right," she told him,"about the flowers.That's why there have been no more checks.After I got back to the hospital,I couldn't get your words out of my mind.So I started buying flowers for the others in the hospital who didn't have any.It gave me such a feeling of joy to see how much they enjoyed them—and from a total stranger.It made them happy,but more than that,it made *me* happy."

"The doctors don't know," she went on,"what is suddenly making me well,but I do! "

Bits & Pieces

几个月后,那位女士又一次来到公墓,看墓人非常惊讶,这一次没人帮她开车,她是自己开车来的。看墓人几乎不敢相信自己的眼睛。

"你说得对,"她对他说,"关于那些花,所以我没有再寄支票来。回到医院后,我始终忘不了你说的每一句话。所以,我开始买花送给医院里那些没有花的病人。看到那些完全不认识的人那么高兴,我也觉得非常欣喜。他们愉快,而我比他们更愉快。"

她接着说:"医生们不知道是什么突然让我恢复了健康,但我知道! "

《零碎》

"That's what I get for stopping to smell the roses."

Reprinted by permission of Jonny Hawkins. ©1998 Jonny Hawkins.

经典系列／光阴的故事

My Mother's Eyes

I remember a period in my childhood when I was absolutely terrified that my mother was going to die.It was the worst thing I could imagine.I worried about it every day.

She seemed to be in good health,but I worried anyway.

My father was a very difficult alcoholic,and the thought of living alone with him was horrifying.

By the time I was fifteen or sixteen,I had grown more independent and the fear subsided.I was confident that I could take care of myself, and could find another place to live,away from my father.So I no longer worried.

And then,when I was eighteen,my mother died.She was only fifty-four.But ironically,her death taught me that sometimes the thing we fear most can turn out to be a blessing.

She had developed a fast-growing,malignant brain tumor that would take her life less than three months after we got the diagnosis.My father had searched frantically for the finest internists,surgeons and oncologists in the world.His wife,he said,would have nothing less than the best medical care money could buy.

But the verdict was unanimous—there was nothing to be done.

There were experimental tests and new chemotherapy treatments, but no one thought they would help.And they didn't. What the doctors did try only made her more sick.

Six weeks before she died,her medical team announced that there

妈妈的眼睛

记得孩提时代有一段时间,非常害怕妈妈死去,这是所能想到的最糟糕的事情,因此每天都在担心。

妈妈身体很好,可我就是放心不下。

爸爸酗酒成性,一想到和他一起生活,真是可怕。

十五六岁时,随着自己的独立,这种恐惧就减弱了。我有信心能照顾自己,可以找另外一个地方生活,远离爸爸,这样就不再担惊受怕了。

18岁时,妈妈去世了,她只有54岁。然而,她的死让我明白,有时一直恐惧的事情也许是件好事。

妈妈得的是恶性脑瘤,它发展得很快,诊断出来不到3个月就夺走了妈妈的生命。爸爸疯狂地寻找世界上最好的内科医生、外科医生和肿瘤医生。他说,他要不惜任何代价,让妻子得到最好的治疗。

但结论是一致的,已经回天乏力了。

尝试了新的检查方法和新的化疗方法,但没有人认为这些会有帮助,也确实没有帮助。医生们的努力只是使她的病情加重。

死前六周,医疗小组宣布再也无能为力。家庭医生建议把她送

was nothing further to do.Our family doctor suggested that she be moved to a nursing home.But she didn't want to go to a nursing home. She wanted to be in her own home.

We agreed,and eventually we brought her home.It was frightening, because we had no idea what would happen to her and how it would affect us.And we didn't have the communication tools we now have to deal with dying and grief.

So we had to rely on our intuition.And we had to trust in the universe.During those weeks,I experienced a peace deep inside me,something beyond my intellect.When I stood back from my fear,my mother's dying began to feel like a natural process.

Years later,I heard someone say,"Dying is absolutely safe." And that is what I instinctively felt during those weeks with my mother.Her body was changing and falling away.I don't know why,but somehow I felt that she was safe.

She ultimately lost the ability to speak.So the house became very quiet as the rest of us spoke in soft,hushed tones.It almost took on the atmosphere of a temple or shrine.

She and her hospital bed and medications had moved into the guest room.There were nurses on duty around the clock.I sometimes avoided going in to see her because I didn't know what to say.The trivial,contrived small talk we often fall into at such times now seemed profane.I gagged on the very thought of meaningless chatter in the face of the most awesome event I had ever witnessed.

One afternoon,I walked in and sat on the edge of her bed.My mother was an elegant,glamorous woman.She seemed so peaceful…

She lay silent and looked at me.I looked at her.I took her hand in mine.She had no energy left,but I felt her squeeze my hand so subtly,so tenderly.I looked deep into her crystal blue eyes.

到私人疗养院，但妈妈不想去那儿，她想留在家里。

最后，我们同意把她送回家。这让人感到害怕，因为我们不知道她会怎样，我们又会受到什么影响。那时，可没有像现在这样对待死亡和悲伤的有效的疏导方法。

所以，我们必须依靠直觉，相信上苍。在这几周里，我感受到了内心深处的平静，是我本无法感受到的平静。当我摆脱恐惧，妈妈的逝世不过是一个自然的过程。

几年后，听到有人说："死亡是绝对安全的。"和妈妈在一起的几个星期里，我本能的感受也是如此。她的身体在改变、在衰退。我不知道原因，可就是认为她会安全的。

终于，妈妈说不出话来了。房屋内寂静下来，每个人说话都低声细语。房子的氛围就像寺庙或圣所。

妈妈、病床和药物都搬到了客人的房间，护士24小时值班。有时，我避免进去见她，因为不知道该如何张口。这时候，琐碎的、刻意的闲谈似乎有渎神意。一想到在这种庄严的场合进行毫无意义的闲谈，我总会哑然无语。

一天下午，我走进房间，坐在妈妈的床边。妈妈高贵典雅，魅力迷人，似乎非常安宁……

她静静地躺着，看着我。我看着她。我把她的手放在自己的手中。她已毫无气力，但仍感到她攥着我的手，如此轻软，如此温柔。我深深地凝视着那双水晶般湛蓝的眼睛。

I kept looking,and as I looked,her eyes got deeper and deeper and deeper.Our eyes locked,and for the next thirty minutes we never diverted our gaze away from each other.We just sat there gazing.And I looked back and back and back,deeper and deeper into her soul.

It was like riding through a tunnel to the core of her soul.And suddenly,there,deep within the withered bulk of a body was the being I knew as my mother.Her love,her care,her nurturing and her compassion all shone through,more radiant than I had ever seen them before.All the barriers between us melted away in the brilliance of the light within her. I sensed that as her body withered,her soul had gained strength.

She squeezed my hand again.And as she did,she gently nodded her head two or three times.In that moment,though not a word had passed between us,I knew that we had said everything that needed to be said.It was okay.She was okay.We loved each other deeply.We honored each other completely.We were grateful for the love we had shared all these years.She would go on,and I would go on,and the place we had touched together would never disappear for either of us.Because somehow,there in her room that day,she and I had shared a glimpse of eternity.

I felt tears,but they were tears of awe more than sadness.And I knew that because I had been willing to go past my horror and fear,to look past her physical deformities and look deeply into her soul,that I had seen her more clearly and contacted her more intimately than ever before.

A few days later,she died.It was a beautiful,peaceful Sunday afternoon.A glorious sunset washed the house in brilliant golden hues, and a warm,gentle breeze soothed and caressed us.A profound aura of peace filled our home.My father,my two sisters and I all held hands around my mother's bed and kissed her good-bye.Then we put our arms around each other and,probably for the first time ever,shared a family

我一直望着,她的目光越来越深邃,越来越深邃。我们目光锁在一起,互相凝望了有30分钟,从未离开过。就坐在那里,互相凝视着。我看着她,看着她,深深地、深深地进入了她的灵魂,就像驶入通向她心灵中心的隧道。突然,在那里,在枯萎的身躯里面,有一个人,就是我所认识的妈妈。她的关心、体恤和怜爱之光照耀进来,比我所见到的任何时候都明亮。我们之间所有的隔阂在她内在的光芒之下悄然融化。我知道,她的身体枯瘦了,可灵魂强大了。

　　妈妈又紧攥了一下我的手。每次这么做时,她都向我点两三下头。那一刻,尽管没有语言的沟通,可我知道这胜过千言万语。一切都会好的。她会好的。我们互相珍爱,互相珍惜,感谢这些天来所体验到的互相给予的爱。她会继续下去,我会继续下去,我们一起呆过的地方永远不会消失。因为不管怎样,那天,在她的房间里,我们分享到了永久的一瞥。

　　我感受到了眼泪,但这不是悲伤的眼泪,是充满崇敬的眼泪。我明白,我终于敢走过恐惧和害怕,看透她病弱的身躯,深入她的灵魂,比以往任何时候都更清楚地了解她,更亲密地接触过她。

　　几天后,一个美丽、宁静的星期天下午。灿烂的余晖用夺目的金色色调洗刷了房屋,温煦的和风抚慰着我们,静谧的气氛填满了房间。爸爸,两个妹妹和我拥在妈妈的床边,向她吻别。然后,我们互相挽着胳臂,这很可能是我们第一次挽着胳臂,享受到家庭的拥抱。我

embrace.We put our heads together and all softly cried.

After a while,we silently moved outdoors.The sun had nearly set, but not quite.And as I looked at it,something occurred to me that I had never noticed before.The sun is most radiant when it's setting.And though it disappears from view,it never dies.

I felt the same about my mother.Like the sun,she had faded from view.But I knew she'd always be with me,even in the darkest of hours.

I looked at my family and marveled at the sense of closeness and intimacy we all felt,at how this moment of wonder and sadness had melted away the walls of separation families often hide behind.For in that moment,the resentments,petty anger and judgments dissolved into the familial love we all shared.We were one consciousness,one heart.My mother,in giving up her own life,had brought the rest of the family together in a closeness and bond that we share to this day.Simultaneously, we felt profound sadness and profound joy.

John E.Welshons

们的头聚拢在一起,轻声哭了起来。

过了一会儿,大家静静地走出门。太阳几乎落了下去,但余晖仍存。看着夕阳,突然想起来,以前从未注意到这些。太阳落山时,更加灿烂耀眼。尽管它会从视线中消失,但永远不会消亡。

母亲不也是这样吗?像太阳一样,她从视野里隐去,但我知道,她永远和我们在一起,即使在最黑暗的时刻。

望着家人,惊诧于大家所感受到的亲近和亲密,惊诧于在这奇妙与悲伤的时刻,隐藏在家庭后面的隔阂之墙是如何融化消失的。在这一刻,仇怨、愤怒和判断力都融化成了互相分享的家庭之爱。我们同一思想、同一条心。妈妈放弃了生命,却给家人带来了亲密的纽带,让我们一直搀挽至今,深深的悲痛和深深的快乐交融在一起。

约翰·E.韦尔绍恩斯

经典系列／光阴的故事

Everybody Can Do Something

CHICKEN SOUP

The basic difference between an ordinary man and a warrior is that a warrior takes everything as a challenge, while an ordinary man takes everything either as a blessing or a curse.

Don Juan

Roger Crawford had everything he needed to play tennis—except two hands and a leg.

When Roger's parents saw their son for the first time, they saw a baby with a thumb-like projection extended directly out of his right forearm and a thumb and one finger stuck out of his left forearm. He had no palms. The baby's arms and legs were shortened, and he had only three toes on his shrunken right foot and a withered left leg, which would later be amputated.

The doctor said Roger suffered from ectodactylism, a rare birth defect affecting only one out of 90,000 children born in the United States. The doctor said Roger would probably never walk or care for himself.

Fortunately Roger's parents didn't believe the doctor.

"My parents always taught me that I was only as handicapped as I wanted to be," said Roger. "They never allowed me to feel sorry for myself or take advantage of people because of my handicap. Once I got into trouble because my school papers were continually late," explained Roger, who had to hold his pencil with both "hands" to write slowly. "I

双语精华版·心灵鸡汤·

天生我才必有用

常人与勇士之根本区别在于，勇士视凡事为挑战，而常人视凡事为福祸。

唐璜

罗杰·克劳福德拥有打网球的一切天赋，只是没有了一双手和一条腿。

罗杰的父母第一眼见到儿子时，这个婴儿从右前臂里直接伸出一个拇指一样的东西，一个拇指和一个从左胳臂里探出的手指。他没有手掌。胳臂和腿都很短。缩短的右脚只有3个趾头。一条干枯的左腿，后来也被截断了。

医生说，罗杰患的是缺指畸形，一种很罕见的生育缺陷，在美国概率为出生婴儿的九万分之一。医生预言，罗杰可能永远也不会行走，照顾自己。

幸运的是，罗杰的父母没有听信医生的话。

"父母总是告诉我，残疾的程度取决于我自己，"罗杰说，"他们决不允许我自我怜悯或者利用自己的缺陷占别人的便宜。有一次，我遇到了一件烦心事，作业总是交得迟，"罗杰解释说，因为他总要用双"手"握住铅笔慢慢写。"我让爸爸给老师写个便条，请求老师允

asked Dad to write a note to my teachers, asking for a two-day extension on my assignments. Instead Dad made me start writing my paper two days early! "

Roger's father always encouraged him to get involved in sports, teaching Roger to catch and throw a volleyball,and play backyard football after school.At age 12,Roger managed to win a spot on the school football team.

Before every game,Roger would visualize his dream of scoring a touchdown.Then one day he got his chance.The ball landed in his arms and off he ran as fast as he could on his artificial leg toward the goal line,his coach and teammates cheering wildly.But at the ten-yard line,a guy from the other team caught up with Roger,grabbing his left ankle. Roger tried to pull his artificial leg free,but instead it ended up being pulled off.

"I was still standing up,"recalls Roger."I didn't know what else to do so I started hopping towards the goal line.The referee ran over and threw his hands into the air.Touchdown! You know,even better than the six points was the look on the face of the other kid who was holding my artificial leg."

Roger's love of sports grew and so did his self confidence.But not every obstacle gave way to Roger's determination.Eating in the lunchroom with the other kids watching him fumble with his food proved very painful to Roger,as did his repeated failure in typing class. "I learned a very good lesson from typing class,"said Roger."You can't do *everything*—it's better to concentrate on what you can do."

One thing Roger could do was swing a tennis racket.Unfortunately, when he swung it hard,his weak grip usually launched it into space.By luck,Roger stumbled upon an odd-looking tennis racket in a sports shop and accidentally wedged his finger between its double-barred handle when he picked it up.The snug fit made it possible for Roger to swing,

许我晚交两天作业。可是爸爸却让我提前两天写作业。"

罗杰的父亲总是鼓励他从事体育活动,教罗杰接发排球,放学后在后院打橄榄球。12岁时,罗杰成功地加入了校橄榄球队。

每场比赛前,罗杰都梦想能底线得分。有一天,机会来了。球落在了他的胳臂中,他竭尽全力迈动假腿朝球门线跑去,教练和队员疯狂地呼喊加油。但是,在十码线时,对方的一个队员追了上来,抓住了他的左膝。罗杰试图把假腿拉拽出来,可最终假腿却被拽掉了。

"我仍然站着,"罗杰回忆道,"只有一个念头,于是就朝球门线一蹦一蹦地跑去。裁判跑过来,手向天空一甩,底线得分!你知道吗,比得6分更有趣的是那个拽住我假腿的家伙脸上惊愕的表情。"

随着罗杰对运动的日益热爱,自信心也增加了。但并不是每一个障碍都会给罗杰的决心让路。中午同其他孩子一起午餐时,让他们看见自己笨手笨脚地吃饭,罗杰感到很苦恼。同样的事情也发生在打字课上。"我从打字课上学到了许多东西,"罗杰说,"你不可能无所不能,最好在所能做的事情上尽自己所能。"

有件事罗杰能做,就是挥动网球拍。不幸的是,只要一使劲,软弱无力的手就握不牢,球拍就会飞向空中。幸运的是,罗杰不经意间在一家运动商店买到了一付外表古怪的球拍,碰巧可以把手指嵌入双杆的把手。有了得心应手的球拍,罗杰就可以像一个强壮的运动

serve and volley like an ablebodied player.He practiced every day and was soon playing—and losing—matches.

But Roger persisted.He practiced and practiced and played and played.Surgery on the two fingers of his left hand enabled Roger to grip his special racket better,greatly improving his game.Although he had no role models to guide him,Roger became obsessed with tennis and in time he started to win.

Roger went on to play college tennis, finishing his tennis career with 22 wins and 11 losses. He later became the first physically handicapped tennis player to be certified as a teaching professional by the United States Professional Tennis Association. Roger now tours the country, speaking to groups about what it takes to be a winner, no matter who you are.

"The only difference between you and me is that you can see my handicap, but I can't see yours. We *all* have them. When people ask me how I've been able to overcome my physical handicaps, I tell them that I haven't overcome anything. I've simply learned what I can't do—such as play the piano or eat with chopsticks—but more importantly, I've learned what I *can* do. Then I do what I can with all my heart and soul."

Jack Canfield

员那样挥舞球拍,发球和凌空击球。他每天都练习打球,不久就会打比赛了,可是一开始时总是输球。

但罗杰并不气馁。他练了又练,打了又打。左手的两个手指做了手术,这样就能更舒服地握紧球拍了,球技也提高了一大步。虽然没有可效仿和指点的榜样,他对网球仍很痴迷,终于开始赢球了。

罗杰上大学时仍然打球,网球生涯结束时赢了22场,输了11场。他成为第1位美国职业网球协会批准的残疾人选手专业教师。罗杰现在参加全国巡回演讲,告诉不同的人群,无论是什么样的人,那些获得成功的要素。

"你我之间唯一的区别在于,你能看见我的残疾,可是我也能看见你的残疾,我们都有残疾。当人们问我怎样能够克服身体残疾时,我告诉他们,我没有克服任何事情,只是学会了做不会做的事情,如弹钢琴,用筷子吃饭。但是更重要的是,学会了自己能做的事情,然后全身心地去做。"

杰克·坎菲尔德

She Was Waiting

Patience is a bitter plant,but it has sweet fruit.

German Proverb

I loved you when you were just an idea,just a dream of future motherhood.I loved planning,wondering what you would look like.It was hart to imagine holding your tiny body,actually creating a little person. Yet I knew that someday you would become a reality,someday my dream of becoming a mother would come true.

When that day came I felt I was dreaming.I couldn't believe you actually were.I rubbed my tummy and talked to you.I thought about your due date,the day that I would actually be able to look at you and hold you,to finally see what look like,my little child. Everything I did,I did for you.Everything I ate,every meal I made,I thought of you,the tiny life that I was feeding.

Your daddy and I planned your room,we picked out names,we started a saving for your future.We already loved you.We couldn't wait to feel your miniature fingers squeezing our own.We looked forward to bathing your soft body,hearing your needy cries for us to nurture you.

We looked forward to your first steps,your first words,your first day at school.We yearned to help you with your homework and to go to your baseball games.It was hard for me to imagine my little child calling the man I love "Daddy." These are the small things we saw in the future during those months that you were growing inside me.We loved you!

她在等待

忍耐是棵苦苗,但可以结出甜蜜果实。

德国谚语

我爱你,在你仅仅是一个动议,一个未来母亲的梦想时,我就爱你。我爱这个计划,不知道将来的你长什么样。很难设想抱着你小小的身体,真真实实地创造出一个小人儿。是的,我知道,有一天这将会成为现实,我要做母亲的梦一定会实现。

当那一天来临,我仿佛身在梦中,我几乎不敢相信你真真切切地存在,我抚摸着肚子和你说话。我想着将来你约定到来的日子,那天,我能真切地看到你、抱着你,知道你长什么样子,我的小宝贝。我做的所有事,每一件都是为你。我吃下去的每一口食物,做的每一顿饭,我都想着你,我正孕育的小小生命。

爸爸和我正筹划着你的房间,为你挑选姓名,为你的未来我们开始节省开支。我们现在已经爱上你了,我们等不及要把你的小手指握在我们的手心里,我们期盼着洗浴你柔软的小身体,听你嗷嗷待哺的哭喊声。

我们盼望着你迈开的第1步,说出的第1个字,上学的第1天。我们渴盼着帮你做家庭作业,陪你打棒球。几乎不能想像我的小小孩儿叫我爱着的那个人"爸爸"。几个月来,只要有你在我体内不断地成长,将来的事在我眼里都微不足道。我们爱你,孩子!

In one minute these dreams were taken from us.On a foggy morning at a routine ultrasound,we found out that you had stopped growing weeks before.You had,in fact,left us without us ever knowing it.All our thoughts and dreams for you had been in vain.But we still loved you! It took a long time to get over this shock.We were told that I could be pregnant again in only a few months.But we wanted *you*!

Eventually we realized that God hadn't meant for us to have a child yet,that we would be more ready when it was meant to be. This comforted us,although we missed you.We had been excited about your arrival,but we could wait if it was meant to be.And we knew that when you did come,I would stay home with you and you would have had a better life,for your daddy would be able to finish school first.In this way,we finally accepted our loss.

It has been four years since that terrible loss.This morning,I sat in our wading pool with my three-year-old daughter.As I watched her tiny hands picking up scoops of water with her bucket,I marveled at her beautiful innocence.It truly was a miracle that we could be part of such a creation.Suddenly she looked at me very intently,and with a twinkle in her eye,she said, "Mommy,you weren't ready for me the first time I came,were you?" I put my arms around my wonderful daughter,and through my tears I could only say, "No,but we missed you very much while you were gone." We no longer have to mourn for our lost baby, for now I know that she has come back to us.This is the same child that we had fallen in love with so many years ago.

Sara Parker

然而那一刻,所有这些梦都离我们而去,那个大雾弥漫的早晨,一次常规的超声波检查让我们发现你在几个星期前已停止生长。事实上你在我们不知不觉中已离我们而去。我们所有的梦想和愿望全都落空了。但是,我们仍然爱你,我们用了很长时间才从这个打击中恢复过来,仅仅几个月前,医生说我可以再孕育一个孩子,但我们要的是你。

最终我们明白了,上帝还没有打算让我们现在就有孩子,我们还需要做更多的准备。这给了我些许的安慰,虽然我们失去了你。我们已经热切地期盼你的到来,但我们还需要等待。而且我们明白,当你真的到来时,我应该待在家里和你在一起,给你更好的生活,你的爸爸也该完成他的学业了。我们这样想也终于接受了失去你的现实。

那可怕的事已过去4年了。今天上午我和3岁大的女儿一起坐在家里的浅水池里,我看着她用小手拿起铲斗舀水。我惊叹于她的天真美丽,我们能够有这样的创造确实是个奇迹。突然,她用那闪闪发光的眼睛专注地看着我说:"妈妈,我第一次来的时候,你们还没有准备好,是吗?"我张开胳膊搂住我令人惊叹的小女儿,透过泪光,说:"不是的,你来的时候,我们恰好错过了。"我们不再为失去的孩子悲伤,因为现在我们已经知道,你已经回到我们身边,你就是许多年前我们爱情的结晶,是同一个孩子。

莎拉·帕克

经典系列／光阴的故事

You Very Good;You Very Fast

At the time,I was living in the Bay Area,and my mother had come to visit for a few days.On the last day of her stay,I was preparing to go out for a run.Working in a very negative environment,I found morning runs very beneficial.As I was going out the door,my mother said, "I don't think running is so hot—that famous runner died."

I started to recount what I had read about Jim Fixx,and how running had probably been the contributing factor to his living far longer than most of the other members of his family,but I knew there was absolutely no point.

As I started running on my favorite trail,I found I couldn't shake her statement.I was so discouraged I could barely run.I began thinking, "Why do I bother to run at all?Serious runners probably think I look ridiculous! I might have a heart attack on the trail—my dad had a fatal heart attack at 50 years old,and he was seemingly in better shape than I am."

My mother's statement hovered over me like a giant blanket.My jog slowed to a walk,and I felt extremely defeated.Here I was in my late 40s,still hoping for an encouraging word from my mother,and equally mad at myself for still seeking an approval that would never come.

Just as I was going to turn around at the two-mile mark and head for home—feeling more discouraged than I could recall in years—I saw an elderly Chinese gentleman walking toward me on the opposite side of the trail.I had seen him walking on other mornings;I had always said, "Good morning," and he had always smiled and nodded his head.This particular morning,he came over to my side of the trail and stood in my

你跑得很棒、很快

我住在海湾地区时，妈妈来看我，住了几天。临走那天我出门去跑步，由于工作的压力，我觉得晨跑非常有益。出门的时候，妈妈说："我不认为跑步有什么好，最著名的马拉松长跑者是跑死的。"

我开始对妈妈谈到曾经读到过得吉姆·菲科斯，他的跑步对他的长寿非常有益，以至使他成为家族中寿命最长的。然而我知道那完全不管用。

当我开始在平时喜爱的道路上跑步时，我发现我推翻不了她的话。我非常沮丧，无法专注地跑步。

我脑子里在想："我为什么要跑步呢？跑步的人可能看起来让人觉得很可笑！可能会在跑道上心脏病发，我父亲是在50岁时发心脏病的，那时他看起来比我还健康。"

母亲的话沉重地压着我，脚步慢下来改为走，感到极度的挫败。我已40多岁，依然希望获得妈妈鼓励的话语，疯狂地追求从未得到的认可。

我在两英里标示牌处转头回家时心情前所未有的糟糕。这时我看到一位年长的中国人从跑道的对面向我走来。其他的早晨我也见过他在此走路。我总是对他说："早上好。"他也总是对我点头微笑。这个特别的早晨，他走到我跑步的这一边挡住我的路。我只好停下

经典系列／光阴的故事

path,forcing me to stop.I was a little miffed.I had let my mother's comment(coupled with a lifetime of similar comments) ruin my day,and now this man was blocking my way.

I was wearing a T-shirt a friend had sent me from Hawaii for Chinese New Year's—it had three Chinese characters on the front,and a scene of Honolulu's Chinatown on the back.Seeing my shirt in the distance had prompted him to stop me.With limited English he pointed to the letters and excitedly said,"You speak?"

CHICKEN SOUP

I told him I didn't speak Chinese,but that the shirt was a gift from a friend in Hawaii.I sensed he didn't understand all of what I was saying,and then,very enthusiastically he said,"Every time see you…you very good…you very fast."

Well,I am neither very good nor very fast,but that day I left with an unexplained bounce in my step.I didn't turn from the trail where my previous dark mood had intended,but continued for six more miles,and you know,for that morning I was very good.I was very fast in my spirit and in my heart.

Because of that little boost I continued to run,and I recently finished my fourth Honolulu Marathon.The New York Marathon is my goal for this year.I know I am never going to win a race,but now,when I get any negative feedback,I think of a kind gentleman who really believed,"You very good…you very fast."

Kathi M.Curry

来,有点恼火。我妈妈的话(以及生活中其他人类似的话)已经把这一天给毁了,而现在这人还要拦住我的路。

我当时穿了一件夏威夷的朋友送我的T恤衫,是中国年的图案,檀香山市唐人街的背景上有3个中国人物。远远地看到我的T恤,他拦住我激动地指着上面的字说:"你会说中文?"

我告诉他我不会说中文,衬衫是夏威夷的朋友送我的。我感觉我说了什么他并没有听懂,但他很热心地说:"每次看到你,你都跑得很棒、很快。"

噢,我跑得不好也不快。但那天余下的时间我感觉脚下出奇地轻快。我故意没有在平时心情不好时转头的地方向回转,而是继续跑了6英里。那天早上我的心情和我的心跳都出奇地好,出奇地快。

小小的赞赏让我坚持跑下去,最近我完成了第4次檀香山市马拉松,今年的下一个目标是纽约马拉松赛。我知道我永远不可能得冠军,但现在如果有人否定我,我就会想到那位好心的中国人,他真诚地认为我跑得很棒、很快。

卡西·M.柯里

Department Store Angel

CHICKEN SOUP

If the doors of perception were cleansed,everything would appear as it is,infinite.

William Blake

I called my eighty-nine-year-old mother early one Friday morning in October to invite her to lunch.Before accepting the invitation,she had to check her calendar to see what activities the retirement home was offering that day.She didn't like to miss anything,whether it was an exercise class,bingo game,a tea with the other residents,a birthday celebration,or any other social activity.She said yes,she would be free from 1:00 to 2:30,but she would like to be home in time to attend the style show.I told her I would pick her up at 1:00 and would have her back by 2:30.

Since my husband and I were leaving the next morning for a week of relaxation in San Diego,I needed to purchase a few last-minute items for the trip,so before picking up my mother I headed to the mall.

I was irritated with myself,knowing I was already feeling rushed and overwhelmed with all that needed to be done for the trip,and then complicating the day even more by making a lunch date with my mother.I had even taken the day off from work so that I could have more time to get ready.There was just too much to do.Maybe I shouldn't have made the lunch plans.Taking the time out for lunch would only interfere with my shopping.I was running late and now I would only have one hour to shop before picking up my mother.I knew though,that

商场天使

如果认知的门被洗涤，一切都会露出它的本来面目，无穷无尽。

威廉·布莱克

10月的一个周五，大清早我给87岁高龄的妈妈打电话，请她吃午餐。她可不愿意错过任何活动：运动课、宾果游戏、茶会、生日聚会，等等。她查看了日程安排和疗养院的活动之后，才说可以。她说从1点到2点半没有安排，但想早点赶回家参加时装表演。我告诉她，1点去接她，2点半送她到家。

我和丈夫第2天早晨要到圣迭戈度一周的假期，必须买度假用的一些物品。在接妈妈前，去了百货商店。

我有些恼火，明知道购物已忙得不可开交，还硬要请妈妈吃午饭。要做的事情太多了，只好请了假，腾出更多的时间准备。我知道，要是不给她打电话见一面，这一周的度假会感到不安。也许本不该做出这样的安排，它只会打乱购物。我动身晚了，只有1个小时购物，然后就得接妈妈。

if I had not called her,I would have felt guilty about leaving for a week in California without seeing her.

As I was walking through a department store I noticed they were having a sale on the black suede,high-top Easy Spirit shoes that I had been looking at for a couple weeks.I took the first chair in a row of about eight,quickly tried them on and decided to purchase them.

"Those looked nice on you.Are they comfortable?"

I looked down the row of chairs,and in the very last one sat a lady about seventy years old.She was just sitting there,looking pretty in her pink blouse,floral skirt,pearl necklace and very sweet smile.She wasn't trying on shoes and it was obvious she was not an employee.

I answered,"Yes,and they are very comfortable."

"Do you think they would be too winter-looking for California?"

"It's funny you should say that,"I replied in a surprised tone of voice,"because I'm leaving for California tomorrow morning."

"You are?"she said. "Well,I'm leaving for California on Monday morning to live in San Diego,even though I've never been to California before."

In a sad voice she proceeded to tell me that her husband passed away earlier that year.They had lived in Cincinnati and in the same house their entire married life.They had one son,and he and his family lived in San Diego.With his encouragement and help,she sold her house along with many of her furnishings,and her most cherished possessions were being delivered to the retirement home in San Diego that her son had chosen. "Oh,that's nice,"I said. "You'll live closer to your son and you can see more of him."

Her voice broke as she said,"But I'm afraid.I've never lived any- where but Cincinnati,and not only am I giving up my home and so many of my belongings,but I'm leaving my friends,too."As she contin- ued her story,she rose from her chair and moved closer to me.We sat

CHICKEN SOUP

双语精华版·心灵鸡汤·

在商场转悠的时候，赶上打折活动，看上一双黑色的小山羊皮、高面的Easy Spirit鞋，我已经找了好几个星期了。我在八连排的第1张椅子上面，急急忙忙地坐下试穿，决定购买。

"你穿这鞋很漂亮，舒服吗？"

我朝椅子的另一面望去，在最后一把椅子上坐着一位70岁左右的老妇人。看起来很漂亮，穿着粉红色的上衣，下配花裙子，戴着珍珠项链，脸上挂着甜甜的笑。她没有试鞋，很显然她不是商场员工。

我回答道："是的，很舒服。"

"你是不是认为，冬天穿它们去加利弗尼亚才合适呢？"

"可真有意思，"我用惊奇的语调回答，"我明天早晨就去加利弗尼亚。"

"真的？"她说，"哦，我星期一早晨要去加利弗尼亚的圣迭戈。我从未去过那里。"

接着，她用难过的语调告诉我，丈夫年初过世了。他们一辈子都住在辛辛那提的家里。他们有一个儿子，住在圣迭戈。在儿子的鼓动和帮助下，她卖掉了自己的房子和大部分的家具，珍贵的家当运到了儿子为她选的圣迭戈的疗养院。"噢，真不错，"我说，"离儿子更近了，可以常看到他。"

她的语气突然一转，说道："但是我有些担心。除了辛辛那提，从未去过任何地方，我不但要放弃家和家具，还要离开朋友。"她从椅子上站起来，挪到我身边，继续讲着她的故事。我们肩并肩地坐着，

down side by side,and I put my shoe box and purse down on the floor.

After listening for a few moments I said, "You know,my eighty-nine-year-old mother lives in a retirement home and she,too,was very apprehensive about making such a big move four years ago."I then told her that my mother and father were married fifty-five years before he passed away.My mother was a homemaker and mother of nine children, so her whole life revolved around her family.There was not much time for social activities other than the times she volunteered to help at church functions.Her life was her family,so when the time came for her to make the decision to sell her home,she was afraid,too.

When she decided on a retirement home,my sisters and I searched for the one closest to us and helped her with the move.   Of course,we were concerned whether she would like that lifestyle.Well,she has enjoyed it from the day she moved in! She is socializing more than she ever has,and the home offers more activities than she can keep up with. The nice part is that they offer so many things,but it is ultimately her choice whether or not to participate in the particular activity offered.I laughed as I told the lady how my mother was involved in so much that she had to check her calendar and squeeze me into her busy schedule for a luncheon date.

This stranger and I talked as if we were friends who had known each other for a long time.After a few minutes we stood up to say good-bye.She thanked me and said she felt much better.I was hesitant to say what I said next,but since I already felt a special kinship with her and sensed a deep spirituality about this lady,I felt it was okay.I turned to her and said,"I believe that God puts certain people in our lives,even if it is for a brief encounter like this,to help us through a difficult time.I don't think this is just a coincidental meeting.I believe it's his way of saying 'It's okay,I'm with you.'

"And I believe he sent us to each other today.You see,I was feeling

双语精华版·心灵鸡汤·

我把鞋盒和钱包放在地上。

听了她的故事，我说："知道吗？我87岁的妈妈也住在养老院里。4年前，她对搬家也是非常恐惧的。"然后，我讲到爸爸是在和妈妈结婚55年后去世的。妈妈一直是个家庭主妇，养育9个儿女，整个生活都围着家庭转。主动在教会帮忙的时间要比参加社交活动的时间多得多。她的生活就是家庭，所以在决定卖掉房子的时候也非常担心。

决定卖掉房子后，我们姐妹找到一处最近的养老院，帮她搬了家。当然，我们担心她是否喜欢那里的生活方式。幸运的是，她从搬进去就喜欢上了它！她参加的活动项目比过去多多了，养老院的安排甚至有点让她抽不出空。当然，最终还是她自己决定参加什么活动。我笑着告诉老妇人，妈妈的日程排得满满的，就连和我约定的午餐都是查看日程安排后硬挤出来的。

陌生的老妇人和我就像是多年的朋友那样聊着天。几分钟过后，我们站起来告别。她谢了我，说她感觉好多了。我正对自己要说的话迟疑不定，但觉得自己与她有着特殊的亲密感，也觉察到她脱俗的气质，就不再犹豫。于是转向她说："相信上帝把一些人安排在我们生活中，即使是像这样短暂的相遇，也是为了帮助我们渡过难关。这不只是一次偶遇，是上帝用它独特的方式说：'不用谢，我与你同在。'"

"我相信，今天是上帝安排我们见面。你看，我今天因为琐事太

overwhelmed with so much to do today,and somewhat irritated that I got myself in a situation that left me with little time to myself.This sharing with you has helped me to appreciate how happy and content my mother is with her new lifestyle,and it makes me more aware of how fortunate I am to still have her with me."

"Oh,"she said,"your mother is so lucky to have you for a daughter. I can see that you love her."

"Yes,and your son loves you so much that he wants you to be closer to him.I'm sure he has chosen a very nice retirement home,and being the pleasant person you are,you won't have any trouble fitting in and making new friends.Besides,San Diego is a beautiful city and you will love the weather."

We stood up and facing each other,held each other's hands."Can I give you a hug for good luck?"I asked.She smiled and nodded.There was a special gentleness in the hug,as if we had known each other a long time.I said,"I'm definitely buying these shoes today,and every time I put them on,I will think of you and say a prayer that all is going well for you." I was at that moment touched by the beauty and warmth about her.Her face seemed to glow.

I bent down to pick up my shoe box and purse.When I stood up,she was gone.How could she disappear so quickly?I looked all around and even walked through the store,hoping to catch one more glimpse of her. But she was nowhere in sight.There are moments in life when we truly sense God's presence,and this was one of those times.I had this feeling that I had been talking with an angel.

I looked at my watch and noticed it was already time to pick up my mother.As I was driving toward my mother's home,deep in thought about this strange yet wonderful encounter,I passed a nursing home with a sign in the yard that read,"The way to feel better about yourself is to make someone else feel better."

多而感觉透不过气来,甚至有点懊恼没给自己留下过多的空暇。刚才跟你的交谈让我欣慰地发现,妈妈新的生活方式是多么快乐和满足,使我更加意识到,有她和我在一起是多么幸运。"

"噢,"她感叹地说,"你妈妈有你这样的女儿可真幸运。我能看出来你爱她。"

"是的。你儿子也非常爱你,他才让你住得离他近些。他选的养老院一定非常好,你又是一个和气的人,会很快融入新的环境,交上新朋友。另外,圣选戈是个美丽的城市,你也会喜欢那儿的天气的。"

我们面对面地站着,握着对方的手。"我可以拥抱你、祝福你吗?"我问道。她笑着点点头。我们的拥抱带有特殊的柔情,就好像我们长久心心相印。我说:"我今天一定会把鞋买下来,每次穿上它,就会想起你,为你祈祷,祝你好运。"此刻,她容光焕发,她的美丽和温柔感动了我。

我弯腰拿起鞋盒和钱包。站起身时,她已经不见了。人怎么会消失得这么快?我四处寻找,甚至走遍整个商场,希望再见着她的身影。但是,她已踪迹难觅。生活中,有时会感到上帝的存在,而这时就是上帝存在的时刻。我有种感觉,我在和天使聊天。

看一下表,已到了接妈妈的时间。在去妈妈家的路上,回想着这次奇妙的邂逅。路过一家小型疗养院,见到院子里的牌子上写着:"自己感觉好的办法是让别人感觉好。"

I pulled into the guest parking spot at my mother's home,feeling suddenly relaxed.I just knew that my mother and I were going to have a most enjoyable afternoon.

Priscilla Stenger

把车停在妈妈家的来宾停车处,突然感觉浑身轻松。我知道,妈妈和我将度过一个非常愉快的下午。

普丽西拉·斯滕格

THE FAMILY CIRCUS®   By Bil Keane

1-22

© 1991 Bil Keane, Inc.
Dist. by Cowles Synd., Inc.

"Stay!"

The Impossible Just Takes a Little Longer

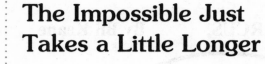

I cannot discover that anyone knows enough to say definitely what is and what is not possible.

Henry Ford

CHICKEN SOUP

At the age of 20,I was happier than I had ever been before in my life.I was active physically:I was a competitive water-skier and snowskier,and played golf,tennis,racquetball,basketball and volleyball.I even bowled on a league.I ran nearly every day.I had just started a new tennis court construction company,so my financial future looked exciting and bright.I was engaged to the most beautiful woman in the world.Then the tragedy occurred—or at least some called it that:

I awoke with a sudden jolt to the sound of twisting metal and breaking glass.As quickly as it all started,it was quiet again.Opening my eyes,my whole world was darkness.As my senses began to return,I could feel the warmth of blood covering my face.Then the pain.It was excruciating and overwhelming.I could hear voices calling my name as I slipped away again into unconsciousness.

Leaving my family in California on a beautiful Christmas evening, I had headed for Utah with a friend of mine.I was going there to spend the rest of the holidays with my fiancée,Dallas.We were to finish our

双语精华版·心灵鸡汤·

暂时的不可能

> 任何人都不能绝对地认定什么是可能，什么是不可能。

亨利·福特

20岁时是我这一生中最幸福的时刻，那时我热爱各种体育运动。我参加滑冰和滑雪比赛。打高尔夫球、壁球、篮球、排球等，甚至还参加一个板球队。我每天跑步。我开始筹建一个网球场建筑公司。从财政收入上说，我的将来是光明的，是令人激动的。我与这个世界上最美丽的姑娘订了婚。就在这时，惨案发生了，至少，人们是这样认为的。

突然的剧烈晃动将我从梦中惊醒，耳边是金属扭曲和玻璃撞碎的声响，接着，又迅速地平静下来，我睁开眼睛，整个世界一片黑暗，随着我的意识逐渐恢复，可以感觉到脸上流淌着温热的血，然后是痛，剧烈的难以忍受的痛。在我再一次失去知觉前，我听到有人叫我的名字。

美丽的圣诞节之夜，我离开加利福尼亚的家人和一个朋友一起去犹他州我的未婚妻达拉斯那儿一起度过余下的假日。我们正在筹

CHICKEN SOUP

upcoming wedding plans—our marriage was to be in five short weeks.I drove for the first eight hours of the trip,then,being somewhat tired and my friend having rested during that time,I climbed from the driver's seat into the passenger seat.I fastened my seat belt,and my friend drove away into the dark.After driving for another hour and a half,he fell asleep at the wheel.The car hit a cement abutment,went up and over the top of it, and rolled down the side of the road a number of times.

When the car finally came to a stop,I was gone.I had been ejected from the vehicle and had broken my neck on the desert floor.I was paralyzed from the chest down.Once I was taken by ambulance to a hospital in Las Vegas, Nevada, the doctor announced that I was now a quadriplegic.I lost the use of my feet and legs.I lost the use of my stomach muscles and two out of my three major chest muscles.I lost the use of my right triceps.I lost most of the use and strength in my shoulders and arms.And I lost the complete use of my hands.

This is where my new life began.

The doctors said I would have to dream new dreams and think new thoughts.They said because of my new physical condition,I would never work again—I was pretty excited about that one,though,because only 93 percent of those in my condition don't work.They told me that I would never drive again;that for the rest of my life I would be completely dependent on others to eat,get dressed or even to get from place to place.They said that I should never expect to get married because···who would want me?They concluded that I would never again play in any kind of athletic sport or competitive activity.For the first time in my young life,I was really afraid.I was afraid that what they said might really be true.

双语精华版·心灵鸡汤·

划即将到来的婚礼,离婚礼只有5个星期了。前半程的8个小时是我开车,感到有些累了,而我的朋友一直在休息。我从驾驶座上下来爬到乘客座,扣牢安全带。我的朋友把车开到夜色里,大约开了一个半小时,他打瞌睡了,车撞到水泥礅上,从上面飞过去滚了几圈,摔下路去。

当车终于停下来,我已经不在车里,我被甩出车外,撞在荒地上摔断了脖子。我从胸部以下没了知觉,当我被救护车送到内华达州拉斯维加斯的一家医院,医生宣布,我已是一名四肢瘫痪者。我不能再使用我的腿和脚,我的腹肌及胸部3块主要肌肉中的两块失去作用,右侧的三头肌麻痹了,同时我的双手几乎完全不能动,双肩和双臂毫无力气,只能有限地活动。

这些改变了我的人生。

医生告诉我要去构思新的梦想,要改变以往的想法。他们说由于我现在的身体状况,我永远不要再工作了。我应该为此感到高兴,因为像我现在这样状况的人中只有93名不必工作。医生告诉我再也不能开车了。从现在起,我的后半生必须完全依靠他人吃饭穿衣,甚至移动一下。我不可能结婚,因为不会有人要我。他们总结说我当然再也不能进行任何体育运动和比赛。对于我年轻的生命来说,这是我第一次感到害怕,害怕医生说的这些成为事实。

While lying in that hospital bed in Las Vegas,I wondered where all my hopes and dreams had gone.I wondered if I would ever be made whole again.I wondered if I would work,get married,have a family and enjoy any of the activities of life that had previously brought me such joy.

During this critical time of natural doubts and fears,when my whole world seemed so dark,my mother came to my bedside and whispered in my ear,"Art,while the difficult takes time … the impossible just takes a little longer."Suddenly a once darkened room began to fill with the light of hope and faith that tomorrow would be better.

Since hearing those words 11 years ago,I am now president of my own company.I am a professional speaker and a published author—*Some Miracles Take Time*.I travel more than 200,000 miles a year sharing the message of The Impossible Just Takes a Little Longer™ to Fortune 500 companies,national associations,sales organizations and youth groups, with some audiences exceeding 10,000 people.In 1992,I was named the Young Entrepreneur of the Year by the Small Business Administration for a six-state region.In 1994,*Success* magazine honored me as one of the Great Comebacks of the Year.These are dreams that have come true for me in my life.These dreams came true not in spite of my circumstances…but,perhaps,because of them.

Since that day I have learned to drive.I go where I want to go and I do what I want to do.I am completely independent and I take care of myself.Since that day,I have had feeling return to my body and have gained back some of the use and function of my right triceps.

I got married to that same beautiful and wonderful girl a year and a half after that fateful day.In 1992,Dallas,my wife,was named Mrs.Utah

CHICKEN SOUP

双语精华版·心灵鸡汤·

躺在拉斯维加斯医院的病床上，我不知道未来在哪里，我所有的梦想都无影无踪。我不知道自己能否恢复，能否工作，能否结婚，能否有家庭，能否再次享受以前带给我那么多愉快的运动人生。

在我最无助最恐惧的时候，在我的世界一片黑暗的时候，我的妈妈来到我的身边，在我耳边说："阿特，困难来临的时候，所有的不可能仅仅只是暂时的。"突然，一片黑暗的房间里充满了希望之光，充满了明天会更好的信念之光。

自从11年前我听到那句话以来，我现在已是一家公司的董事长，职业演说家，并写作出版了《假以时日，创造奇迹》一书。

我每年行程20万英里把"不可能只是暂时的"这种信念和信息传输给世界500强企业、给民族联合会和某些营销组织和青年联合会，有时听众可达上万人。1992年，六州联合会的小型工商企业管理局评选我为当年的青年企业家。1994年《成功者》杂志给了我当年最成功康复称号。这些是我这一生的梦想，它们已经成为现实。尽管我有这样那样的现状，这些梦想还是实现了，也许这样的现状也是梦想成真的起因。

自从我学会了开车那天起，我去了所有要去的地方，做了所有想做的事，我能够照顾自己，完全独立。从那天起，我丢失的情感回来了，我还找回了右侧三头肌的部分功能。

在我发生事故一年半后，我和原来那位美丽可爱的未婚妻结婚了。1992年，达拉斯，我的妻子获犹他州第一夫人称号，也是第3届的

and was third runner-up to Mrs.USA! We have two children—a three-year-old daughter named McKenzie Raeanne and a one-month-old son named Dalton Arthur—the joys of our lives.

I have also returned to the world of sports.I have learned to swim, scuba dive and parasail—as far as I know I am the first quadriplegic of record to parasail.I have learned to snow ski.I have also learned to play full-contact rugby.I figure they can't hurt me any worse! I also race wheelchairs in 10Ks and marathons.On July 10,1993,I became the first quadriplegic in the world to race 32 miles in seven days between Salt Lake City and St.George,Utah—probably not one of the brightest things I have ever done,but certainly one of the most difficult.

Why have I done all of these things?Because a long time ago I chose to listen to the voice of my mother and to my heart rather than to the concourse of dissenting voices around me,which included medical professionals.I decided that my current circumstances did not mean I had to let go of my dreams.I found a reason to hope again.I learned that dreams are never destroyed by circumstances;dreams are born in the heart and mind,and only there can they ever die.Because while the difficult takes time,the impossible just takes a little longer.

Art E. Berg

美国夫人亚军。我们有两个孩子，3岁的女儿摩肯妮·丽安妮和1个月大的儿子道尔顿·亚瑟。他们是我们生活的乐趣。

我也已回到运动的世界里。我学会了游泳、潜水、帆伞等运动。我甚至创造了第一个四肢瘫痪运动员的帆伞纪录。我学会了滑雪，也学会打全场橄榄球。我相信再怎么受伤也不会比现在还严重。我也参加轮椅10公里赛跑及马拉松比赛。1993年7月10日举办了从盐湖城至圣·乔治之间32英里的残疾人世界越野赛。该赛事需7日内完成，我获四肢瘫痪组第1名。我几乎做过所有犹他州最辉煌的事，当然也是最困难的事。

我为什么要做这些呢？因为很久之前，我选择了听取我妈妈的声音，而不是去听那些我周围大部分人的说法，也包括那些医疗专家的说法。我作出决定，那就是我目前的状况不代表一定要放弃梦想。我找到了重新抱有希望的理由。我知道任何恶劣环境永远都不能击碎梦想。因为梦想生长在我们心中，在我们思想里。只有从心里放弃，它才会消亡。因为当困难到来的时候，一切的不可能仅仅只是暂时的。

阿特·E. 博格

Wrestling

Her chocolate curls obeyed the rhythm of her dancing feet,as she twisted and bounded on limber toes beside me all the way to my classroom.Once inside,I pulled out the materials I would need to evaluate the learning problems of this spunky little first grader. She sat there,skinny legs swinging wildly under her chair to the cadence of some jump-rope chant she was humming under her breath.Her bottom lip reached up to recover a small crumbly remnant of lunch as she grabbed the pencil I placed in front of her.Big eyes,eager to please and full of mischief, smiled at me as I began to recite the spelling words.

"Big.The big dog jumped over the wagon.Big." I watched as she struggled with her pencil grip and scratched out a "d" for a "b" and a "6" for a "g"."That un's wrong too,huh?" I watched the light in her smiling eyes fade word by word to dreary surrender. She scowled at her little hands,as though she was scolding them for their misbehavior.I winced,suddenly very doubtful for my purpose and decency.Time paused for a moment as we sat there in silence,pondering our predicament.Then, very unexpectedly,those little feet that had hung there so lonely for a dance recovered their rhythm.She banished the pencil from her hand and produced a grin so intense with mischief and sport that it startled me.

"Ya wanna wrestle?" she invited.My bewildered gaze was met with a challenging grin.Slow to catch on,I repeated her query, "What?Do I want to wrestle?" She was not about to leave me with such a humble impression of her talents.Her invitation announced what she was good at—wrestling.

After some negotiating she settled on four matches of arm

摔跤

她从我身边走过,直奔向教室。身体左右扭动,脚灵活地打着拍子,红褐色的头发随脚步舞动着。走进教室,我就拿出材料。这些是用来分析这个瘦小却胆量十足的一年级学生学习困难的原因的。她坐在那儿,哼着某个跳绳的旋律,纤瘦的腿在桌子下面大幅摆动。下嘴唇抿上来,盖住午餐留在嘴上的残迹。同时,紧紧握住我放在她面前的铅笔。眼睛大大的,热切、迷人、顽皮、满含笑意。我开始朗读要拼写的单词。

"大,一条大狗越过马车,大。"我看她费力地握着笔,钩钩抹抹地写出来,把字母"b"写成了"d",把字母"g"写成了数字"6"。"这个拼得也不对,喂?"我说出一个她拼错的词,她笑眼中的光亮就暗淡一些,直到笑意全消,露出郁闷的目光。她怒视着自己的小手,好像在责备它们不争气。突然间,我对自己这次评价的目的和合理性产生了怀疑,心里打起了退堂鼓。时间暂时像停顿了一样,我们坐在那里,一言不发,各怀心事。出乎意料的是,那双孤独地垂在那里等待舞蹈的小脚,恢复了韵律。她把铅笔一扔,露出笑容,笑容中透露出顽皮。她的举动把我吓了一跳。

"想摔跤吗?"她挑战道。我迷惑地看着她那充满挑衅的微笑,没明白她的意思,就重复着她的问话:"什么?想摔跤?"给我留下无能的印象,这是她决计不会答应的。她的挑战宣布了她的长项:摔跤。

经过一番协商,确定进行4回合摔跤比赛,每比一场就拼写一个

经典系列／光阴的故事

wrestling,one for each remaining spelling word.And when we were fin-ished she skipped out of my classroom boasting a winning record.Her gentle yet pointed appraisal of my testing etiquette left me contrite yet resolved to level out the playing field.I instituted some new rules.Rule one:It is illegal to use learning difficulties as an excuse to sneak up on young learners and rob them of giggles and dancing feet.Rule two:If I ever forget rule one,I must spend an entire recess in the middle of a dodgeball circle,surrounded by sixth-graders.

Renee Adolph

剩下的单词。比赛结束了,她蹦蹦跳跳地跑出教室,到处吹嘘获胜记录,还对我的比赛风度进行了温和而率真的评价,我有些懊悔,于是决心让比赛变得公正一些。为此,制订了一些新规则。规则1:禁止把学生学习困难当做借口接近学生,剥夺他们的笑声和舞步。规则2:如果我忘记了规则1,整个课间玩躲球游戏时,就必须站在六年级学生围成的大圈中间,任他们朝我身上掷球。

勒妮·阿道夫

"There must be another way to record
attendance for our services."

The Power Of Optimism

The years of the Vietnam War were a confused troubled time for American foreign policy, making the suffering of the participants all the more tragic. But out of it has come the marvelous story about Captain Gerald L. Coffee.

His plane was shot down over the China Sea on February 3, 1966, and he spent the next seven years in a succession of prison camps. The POWs who survived, he says, did so by a regimen of physical exercise, prayer and stubborn communication with one another. After days of torture on the Vietnamese version of the rack, he signed the confession they demanded. Then he was thrown back into his cell to writhe in pain. Even worse was his guilt over having cracked. He did not know if there were other American prisoners in the cell block, but then he heard a voice:"Man in cell number 6 with the broken arm, can you hear me?"

It was Col. Robinson Risner."It's safe to talk.Welcome to Heartbreak Hotel,"he said.

"Colonel,any word about my navigator,Bob Hansen?"Coffee asked.

"No.Listen,Jerry,you must learn to communicate by tapping on the walls.It's the only dependable link we have to each other."

Risner had said "We"! That meant there were others."Thank god, now I'm back with the others,"Coffee thought.

"Have they tortured you,Jerry?"Risner asked.

"Yes,And I feel terrible that they got anything out of me."

"Listen,"Risner said, "once they decide to break a man,they do it. The important thing is how you come back.Just follow the Code.Resist to the utmost of your ability.If they break you,just don't stay broken. Lick your wounds and bounce back.Talk to someone if you can.Don't

双
语
精
华
版
·
心
灵
鸡
汤
·

信念的力量

越南战争那几年,美国外交政策混乱不堪,麻烦不断。卷入战争的人们上演了一幕幕惨痛的悲剧。期间,发生在杰拉尔德·L·科菲身上的故事更是令人感慨不已。

1966年2月,科菲的飞机在中国海上空被击落。之后7年,他是在一个又一个战俘集中营中度过的。他说,生存下来的战俘都是靠锻炼身体、祈祷和坚持不懈的互相交流挺过来的。经过几天越南式行刑台的折磨,科菲按照他们的要求,在自白书上签字后被投回牢房,任其痛苦地翻滚。更糟糕的是,他担心自己精神会崩溃。不知道在牢房里是否还有其他的美国战俘, 这时他听到了一个声音:"6号牢房的断臂人,能听见我说的话吗?"

这是罗宾逊·里斯纳上校。"谈话没有危险。欢迎来到伤心旅馆。"他说。"上校,知道飞行员鲍伯·汉森的消息吗?"科菲问道。

"不知道。听着,杰里,你必须拍打墙壁与人沟通,这是我们相互唯一的联系网。"

里斯纳说了"我们"!意味着还有其他人。"感谢上帝,现在又回到大家当中了。"科菲想。

"折磨你了吧,杰里?"里斯纳问。

"是的,从我身上套出话来才是可怕的呢。"

"听着,"里斯纳说,"一旦他们决定摧毁一个人,就决不手软。能够回来,这才是重要的。牢记乐观的信条,尽自己所能抵抗到底。如果他们弄折了你,不要听之不管。要舔好伤口进行反击。可能的话就

get down on yourself.We need to take care of one another."

For days at a time Coffee would be punished for some minor infraction by being stretched on the ropes.His buddy in the next cell would tap on the wall,telling him to "hang tough,"that he was praying for him."Then,when he was being punished,"Coffee says,"I would be on the wall doing the same for him."

At last Coffee received a letter from his wife:

> *Dear Jerry,*
>
> *It has been a beautiful spring but of course we miss you.The kids are doing great.Kim skis all the way around the lake now.The boys swim and dive off the dock,and little Jerry splashes around with a plastic bubble on his back.*

Coffee stopped reading because his eyes were filling with tears as he clutched his wife's letter to his chest."Little Jerry?Who's Jerry?"Then he realized.Their baby,born after his imprisonment,had been a son and she had named him Jerry.There was no way she could know that all her previous letters had been undelivered,so she talked about their new son matter-of-factly.Coffee says:

"Holding her letter, I was full of emotions: relief at finally knowing that the family was well, sorrow for missing out on Jerry's entire first year, gratitude for the blessing of simply being alive."The letter concluded:

> *All of us, plus so many others, are praying for your safety and return soon. Take good care of yourself, honey.*
> *I love you.*
>
> > *Bea*

Coffee tells about the long, long hours during which the prisoners

和人谈话,不要自行消沉,我们需要互相照顾。"

每隔几天,科菲就会因细小的违纪而受到五马分尸般的折磨。遇到这种情况,隔壁牢房的狱友就会拍打墙壁,告诉他"坚强一些",说他正在为科菲祈祷。"后来,当他受折磨的时候,"科菲说,"我也会敲打墙壁鼓励他。"

终于,科菲收到了妻子的来信:

> 亲爱的杰里:
>
> 又是一个春暖花开的时节,我们真的很想念你。孩子们表现的都很棒。吉姆能绕着湖一直滑雪下来。儿子们游泳时,可以从码头上往下跳水。小杰里爱背着游泳圈在水里乱扑腾。

科菲读不下去了,眼里盈满了泪水。他把信紧紧地贴在胸前。"小杰里?他是谁?"不久,意识到这是他们的孩子。在他被囚禁之后出生的是个男孩,妻子给他起名叫杰里。她根本不知道以前写的信杰里都没有收到,所以还以一种熟稔的口气称呼小杰里。

科菲说:"捧着她的信,我百感交集。让我放心的是知道了家里人一切平安;让我难过的是小杰里周岁的一整年都错过了;让我感激的是我受到保佑仍然活着。"信的结尾是:

> 我们家所有的人,还有其他人,正为你的安全归来祈祷。照顾好自己,宝贝。
>
> 爱你的
>
> 碧

科菲讲道,狱友们会好几个小时地在脑海里像过电影一样闪现

played movies in their minds, of going from room to room in their houses back home, the camera taking in every detail. Over and over they played scenes of what it was going to be like to be back. Coffee says it was his friends and his faith that helped him through. Every Sunday the senior officer in each cell block would pass a signal—church call. Every man stood up in his cell, if he was able, and then with a semblance of togetherness, they would recite the Twenty-Third Psalm: "Thou prepares"a table before me in the presence of mine enemies, thou anointest my head with oil; my cup runneth over."

Coffee says:"I realized that despite being incarcerated in this terrible place,it was my cup that runneth over because someday,however, whenever,I would return to a beautiful and free country."

Finally,the peace treaty was signed,and on February 3,1973,the seventh anniversary of his capture,Coffee was called before two young Vietnamese officers.

"Today it is our duty to return your belongings,"one said.

"What belongings?"he asked.

"This."

He swallowed hard and reached for the gold wedding band the soldier held between his thumb and forefinger.Yes,it was his.He slipped it onto his finger.A little loose,but definitely his ring.He had never expected to see it again.

[My] kids were 11 or 12 years old when my ring had been taken away.Suddenly I felt old and weary.During the prime years of my life,I had sat in a medieval dungeon,had my arm screwed up,had contracted worms and God knows what else.I wondered if my children,now older and changed so much,would accept me back into the family and what our reunion would be like.And I thought of Bea.Would I be okay for her?Did she still love me?Could she possibly know how much she had meant to me all these years?

The bus trip to the Hanoi airport was a blur,but one thing stood out

家里的场景,从一个房间到另一个房间,镜头摄入了每个细节,一遍又一遍地放映着回家时的一幕幕情景。科菲说,是狱友和信念让他渡过难关。每到星期日,牢房里的长官会发出教堂铃声般的号令,如果能的话,每个人都要在牢房里站起来,异口同声地背诵第23篇《诗篇》:"在我敌人面前,你为我摆设筵席。你对我的头施以涂油礼,使我的福杯满溢。"

科菲说:"我意识到,尽管被监禁在这暗无天日的地方,但是我的福杯满溢,终究有一天,我会回到美丽、自由的祖国。"

终于,和平协议签署了。1973年2月,科菲被捕的第7年,他被叫到两名年轻越南军官面前。

"今天,我们该归还你的东西了。"一位军官说。

"什么东西?"科菲问道。

"这个。"

科菲吃惊地倒吸了一口气,伸手去拿军官拇指和食指之间的结婚戒指。是的,这是他的戒指。他把戒指戴在手上,有点松,但确定无疑是他的。他从未想到会再次见到这枚戒指。

"孩子十一二岁的时候,戒指被夺走了。我一夜之间衰老了。在人生的黄金年代,我却蹲在中世纪的监牢。胳臂被扭歪了,感染了寄生虫病,天晓得还有什么灾病。我急切地想知道,现在孩子们已经长大了,也改变了许多,能否接受我,团圆的情景会如何呢?我想起了碧,她还能接纳我吗?她还爱我吗?能否知道这么多年她对我意味着什么吗?"

乘车到河内机场的记忆已经模糊,但科菲却清楚地记得一件事

with clarity for Coffee:The bright beautiful,red,white,and blue flag painted on the tail of the enormous Air Force C-141 transport that gleamed in the sun,awaiting the first load of freed prisoners.

Next to the aircraft were several dozen American military people who smiled at them through the fence and gave them the thumbs-up signal.As they lined up by twos,the Vietnamese officer reeled off their names,rank and service.

"Commander Gerald L. Coffee,United States Navy."(He had been promoted two ranks in his absence.)

As Coffee stepped forward,his attention was riveted on an American colonel wearing crisp Air Force blues, wings and ribbons. It was the first American military uniform he had seen in many years. The colonel returned Coffee's brisk salute.

"Commander Gerald L. Coffee reporting for duty, sir."

"Welcome back,Jerry."The colonel reached forward with both hands and shook Coffee's hand.When the plane was loaded,the pilot taxied directly onto the runway without holding short,then locked the brakes and jammed his throttles forward.The huge beast rocked and vibrated as the pilot made his final checks of the engine's performance. The roar was horrendous as the brakes were released and they lurched forward on the runway.When they were airborne,the pilot's voice came onto the speaker and filled the cabin.It was a strong,sure voice.

"Congratulations,gentlemen.We've just left North Vietnam."Only then did they erupt into cheers.

The first leg of their trip home took them to Clark Air Force Base in the Philippines. The crowd held up banners:"Welcome Home! We love you. God bless."From behind the security lines they applauded wildly as the name of each debarking POW was announced. There were television cameras, but the men had no idea that at that very moment in the small hours of the morning, millions of Americans back home were riveted to their television sets, cheering and weeping.

情:在阳光下闪耀的空军C-141运输机的尾部,涂着一面鲜艳美丽的红白蓝相间的旗子,正等待着装载第一批释放的战俘。

飞机旁,站着几十个美国军人,隔着围栏朝他们微笑,向他们竖起大拇指。战俘们两人一排,越南军官叫着他们的名字、军衔和军种。

"杰拉尔德·L.科菲中校,美国海军。"(在服刑期间他被提升了两级)。

科菲跨步走到前面,目光集中在一位美国上校身上,他穿着挺括的蓝色空军制服,挂着徽章和绶带。这是科菲这么多年后第一次看见美国军装。上校轻快地给科菲回了个军礼。

"杰拉尔德·L.科菲中校报到,先生。"

"欢迎回来,杰里。"说完,上校双手握住了科菲的手。当人们走上飞机,飞行员一刻没有停留,直接把飞机滑进跑道,然后将飞机刹住并用力向前推动油门。当飞行员最后一次检查发动机的性能时,这个庞然大物摇动着,颤动着。刹车松开后,伴随着巨大的轰鸣声,飞机在跑道上向前冲去。飞到空中,飞行员的声音透过麦克风,传遍了整个机舱,果断而有力。

"先生们,祝贺你们。我们刚刚飞离北越。"人们爆发出了欢呼声。

返乡的第一站是菲律宾的克拉克空军基地。人们举起了旗子:"欢迎回家!我们爱你们!上帝保佑你们。"当走下飞机的每个战俘的名字被宣布时,站在警戒线后的人们就狂热地鼓掌欢呼。但战俘们却不知道的是,借助于摄像机的帮助,就在此刻,这短短的早上几个小时中,数以百万的美国人正在家里,聚精会神地看着电视,欢呼着,哭泣着。

Special telephones had been set up to accommodate their initial calls home. Coffee's stomach churned as he waited the interminable few seconds for Bea to pick up the phone in Sanford, Florida, where she and the children were waiting.

"Hello, babe. It's me. Can you believe it?"

"Hi,honey.Yes.We watched you on TV when you came off the airplane.I think everybody in America saw you.You look great! "

"I dunno.I'm kinda scrawny.But I'm okay.I'm just anxious to get home."

After his long-awaited reunion with his wife and children,he and his family attended mass the following Sunday.Afterwards,in response to the parish priest's welcome,here is what Coffee said.It summarizes as well as anything I know of the optimist's code:

"Faith was really the key to my survival all those years.Faith in myself to simply pursue my duty to the best of my ability and ultimately return home with honor.Faith in my fellow man,starting with all of you here,knowing you would be looking out for my family,and faith in my comrades in those various cells and cell blocks in prison,men upon whom I depended and who in turn depended upon me,sometimes desperately.Faith in my country,its institutions and our national purpose and cause … And,of course,faith in God—truly,as all of you know, the foundation for it all … Our lives are a continuing journey—and we must learn and grow at every bend as we make our way,sometimes stumbling,but always moving,toward the finest within us."

David McNally

From The Power of Optimism

by Alan Loy McGinnis

为了方便战俘们给家打第1个电话，专用电话机已经搭了起来。在科菲看来，等待碧接电话的几秒钟，竟如此漫长。他心潮起伏。碧和孩子们正在遥远的佛罗里达州的桑福德等待着他的电话。

"你好，宝贝。是我，你能相信这是真的吗？"

"你好，亲爱的。是的，我相信。在电视上看见你走下飞机。我想，美国的每个人都看见了你。你看起来不错！"

"我不知道，就是有点虚弱，但是没问题。我很想回家。"

经过漫长的等待，科菲和妻儿团聚了。第1个星期日，他们一起参加了弥撒。为了答谢教区牧师的欢迎，科菲说出了下面的话，总结起来就是很好的乐观主义信条。

"信念确实是我这么多年生存下来的关键。在自己身上，信念就是恪守职责，荣归故里；在同伴身上，包括在场的每个人，信念就是知道你们会照顾我的家庭；在那些被关在牢狱的战友们身上，信念就是我们可以互相依靠，义无反顾；当然，在上帝身上，正如你们所知，信念就是一切的根基……生命是永不停止的旅行，在每一处弯道，都必须学习和成长。有时会踉跄而行，但我们要一直向前，直至心中最后的终点。"

大卫·麦克纳利

选自阿兰·洛伊·麦金尼斯的《信念的力量》

A Little Girl's Dream

The promise was a long time keeping.But then,so was the dream.

In the early 1950s in a small Southern California town,a little girl hefted yet another load of books onto the tiny library's counter.

The girl was a reader.Her parents had books all over their home, but not always the ones she wanted.So she'd make her weekly trek to the yellow library with the brown trim,the little one-room building where the children's library actually was just a nook.Frequently,she ventured out of that nook in search of heftier fare.

As the white-haired librarian hand-stamped the due dates in the 10-year-old's choices,the little girl looked longingly at "The New Book" prominently displayed on the counter.She marveled again at the wonder of writing a book and having it honored like that,right there for the world to see.

That particular day,she confessed her goal.

"When I grow up," she said,"I'm going to be a writer.I'm going to write books."

The librarian looked up from her stamping and smiled,not with the condescension so many children receive,but with encouragement.

"When you do write that book," she replied,"bring it into our library and we'll put it on display,right here on the counter."

The little girl promised she would.

As she grew,so did her dream.She got her first job in ninth grade, writing brief personality profiles,which earned her $1.50 each from the local newspaper.The money palled in comparison with the magic of seeing her words on paper.

双语精华版·心灵鸡汤·

小女孩的梦想

承诺需要长时间的坚持,梦亦如此。

20世纪初,在加利弗尼亚南部的一个小镇,一个小女孩费力地又把一摞书放在窄小的图书柜台上。

这个女孩是位小读者,家里父母的书摆满厅堂,可那些并不是她想要的书。于是,她每周一次徒步来到图书馆。这个图书馆其实只是一个黄色的小房子,有棕色的贴面。儿童图书摆放在一个小角落里。小女孩经常走出角落,大胆地寻找更有营养的精神食粮。

白发苍苍的图书馆员在这个10岁女孩选的书上用手戳盖上归还日期,小女孩满脸渴望地盯着摆在柜台显著位置的"新书"。写书给世界看,受到如此的尊重,让她惊羡不已。

在一个特别的日子,她袒露了自己的目标。

"我长大,"她雄心勃勃地说,"要成为一名作家。我要写书。"

正在盖戳的图书馆员抬起头来,笑了,一改往日居高临下的姿态,鼓励道:"你要是写完了,一定给我们图书馆送来。我们要把它展示在新书柜台上。"

小女孩许下誓言,一定送来新书。

随着年龄的增长,这个梦越来越强烈。九年级时,她有了第1份工作,给当地的报纸写人物简介,每写一份,可挣150美元。看到自己的文章出现在报纸上,这份神奇让金钱黯然失色。

A book was a long way off.

She edited her high-school paper, married and started a family, but the itch to write burned deep. She got a part-time job covering school news at a weekly newspaper. It kept her brain busy as she balanced babies.

But no book.

She went to work full-time for a major daily. Even tried her hand at magazines.

Still no book.

Finally, she believed she had something to say and started a book. She sent it off to two publishers and was rejected. She put it away, sadly. Several years later, the old dream increased in persistence. She got an agent and wrote another book. She pulled the other out of hiding, and soon both were sold.

But the world of book publishing moves slower than that of daily newspapers, and she waited two long years. The day the box arrived on her doorstep with its free author's copies, she ripped it open. Then she cried. She'd waited so long to hold her dream in her hands.

Then she remembered that librarian's invitation, and her promise.

Of course, that particular librarian had died long ago, and the little library had been razed to make way for a larger incarnation.

The woman called and got the name of the head librarian. She wrote a letter, telling her how much her predecessor's words had meant to the girl. She'd be in town for her 30th high school reunion, she wrote, and could she please bring her two books by and give them to the library? It would mean so much to that ten-year-old girl, and seemed a way of honoring all the librarians who had ever encouraged a child.

The librarian called and said, "Come." So she did, clutching a copy of each book.

She found the big new library right across the street from her old

然而,书还是遥遥无期。

她给学校当编辑、结婚、建立家庭,但写作的欲望愈烧愈旺。她在一家周报获得了兼职工作,报道学校新闻,加上照顾孩子,已忙得不可开交。

书还是没有影子。

她在一家大型日报担任了全职工作,甚至在杂志上也一试身手。

可就是没有书。

终于,她发现有话要说,开始写书。完成后,把书稿寄给两家出版社,都被拒绝了。她悲伤地把书稿搁置起来。几年来,久远的梦想一直执著地跟随,日渐强烈。她找了个经纪人,开始写另外一本书,还把第1本书翻了出来,不久两本书稿都卖了出去。

但是书籍出版界运转的步伐比日报界慢多了,她足足等了两年。那天,当邮件到来时,她迫切地拆开盒子,看到里面免费赠送作者的样书时,她哭了。她用了如此之久的时间把握梦想。

然后,她想起来图书馆员让她送书的事情和自己的承诺。

当然,当年的图书馆员早已过世,小小的图书馆也已被夷为平地,取代它的是一座大型建筑。

她打电话得到了图书馆长的名字,就写信给图书馆长。讲述了前任图书馆长的话对她不同寻常的影响。她写到,要回到小镇参加高中30周年聚会,能否把她写的两本书赠送给图书馆?这对当年那个10岁的孩子意义重大,也是对所有鼓励过她的人的一种感激。

图书馆长打电话说:"过来吧。"她就去了,带着她的两本书。

她发现,这座大而新的图书馆与她的高中一路之隔,正好在她

high school; just opposite the room where she'd struggled through algebra, mourning the necessity of a subject that writers would surely never use, and nearly on top of the spot where her old house once stood, the neighborhood demolished for a civic center and this looming library.

Inside, the librarian welcomed her warmly. She introduced a reporter from the local newspaper—a descendant of the paper she'd begged a chance to write for long ago.

Then she presented her books to the librarian, who placed them on the counter with a sign of explanation. Tears rolled down the woman's cheeks.

Then she hugged the librarian and left, pausing for a picture outside, which proved that dreams can come true and promises can be kept. Even if it takes 38 years.

The ten-year-old girl and the writer she'd become posed by the library sign, right next to the reader board, which said:

WELCOME BACK,
JANN MITCHELL

Jann Mitchell

的教室对面。在那个教室里,她费力地解过代数题,也曾为要写毫不相干的题目而愁眉不展过。几乎就在原地上,拆掉了所有的建筑,建起了市中心区和这个赫然耸立的图书馆。

进入图书馆,馆员热情地接待了她,向她介绍了当地的一家报社的记者。这家报社是由很多年前她恳求为之写作的那家报社发展起来的。

她把新书赠送给了图书馆员。图书馆员把书放在新书书架上,并附上说明文字。眼泪滚落在她的两颊。

她拥抱了图书馆员,然后起身离开。在门口照了张相,为了证明梦可以实现,诺言可以兑现,即使用上38年的时间。

当年的10岁小女孩,现在成了作家,在图书馆的标识旁摆好了姿势照相,正好挨着读者告知板,上面写着:

欢迎回来,
詹恩·米切尔

詹恩·米切尔

The Story of Margaret and Ruth

We are each of us angels with only one wing.And we can only fly embracing each other.

Luciano De Creschenzo

In the spring of 1983,Margaret Patrick arrived at the Southeast Senior Center for Independent Living to begin her physical therapy.As Millie McHugh,a long-time staff member,introduced Margaret to people at the center,she noticed the look of pain in Margaret's eyes as she gazed at the piano.

"Is anything wrong?" asked Millie.

"No," Margaret said softly."It's just that seeing a piano brings back memories.Before my stroke,music was everything to me." Millie glanced at Margaret's useless right hand as the black woman quietly told some of the highlights of her music career.

Suddenly Millie said,"Wait right here.I'll be back in a minute." She returned moments later,followed closely by a small,white-haired woman in thick glasses.The woman used a walker.

"Margaret Patrick," said Millie,"meet Ruth Eisenberg."Then she smiled. "She too played the piano,but like you,she's not been able to play since her stroke. Mrs.Eisenberg has a good right hand,and you have a good left,and I have a feeling that together you two can do something wonderful."

"Do you know Chopin's Waltz in D flat?" Ruth asked. Margaret nodded.

Side by side,the two sat on the piano bench.Two healthy hands—

双语精华版·心灵鸡汤·

玛格丽特和露思的故事

> 我们都是只有一只翅膀的天使，我们只能互相拥抱着起飞。

卢西亚诺·德·克里斯琴佐

1983年的春天，玛格丽特·帕特里克来到东南康复中心独立生活，并开始接受物理治疗。当米莉·麦休，中心的长期职员把她介绍给其他人时，她注意到玛格丽特看到钢琴时眼中流露出的悲伤。

"怎么了？"米莉问。

"没什么。"玛格丽特轻轻说："只是因为看见了钢琴，引起我许多回忆。出事前，音乐就是我的一切。"在这位黑人妇女静静地叙述她以前的音乐生涯中的精彩之处时，靡丽盯着她残疾的右手。

突然，米莉说："等一等，我马上回来。"她回来时后面紧紧跟着一位个子矮矮的、头发花白、戴着厚厚镜片的眼镜的女士，这位女士挂着拐杖。

"玛格丽特·帕特里克，"米莉说，"这是露思·埃森博格。"她笑着说："她也弹钢琴，但和你一样，出事之后不能弹了，埃森博格夫人有一只健全的右手，而你有正常的左手，我有个想法，这两只手结合起来，一定能演绎出美妙的音乐。"

"你知道肖邦的华尔兹D大调吗？"露思问，玛格丽特点点头。

肩并着肩，两人坐在琴凳上，两只健康的手——一只具有修长、

one with long,graceful black fingers,the other with short,plump white ones—moved rhythmically across the ebony and ivory keys.Since that day,they have sat together over the keyboard hundreds of times—Margaret's helpless right hand around Ruth's back,Ruth's helpless left hand on Margaret's knee,while Ruth's good hand plays the melody and Margaret's good hand plays the accompaniment.

Their music has pleased audiences on television,at churches and schools,and at rehabilitation and senior-citizen centers.And on the piano bench,more than music has been shared by these two.For it was there, beginning with Chopin and Bach and Beethoven,that they learned they had more in common than they ever dreamed—both were great-grand-mothers and widows (Margaret's husband died in 1985),both had lost sons,both had much to give,but neither could give without the other.

Sharing that piano bench,Ruth heard Margaret say,"My music was taken away,but God gave me Ruth."And evidently some of Margaret's faith has rubbed off on Ruth as they've sat side by side these past five years,because Ruth is now saying,"It was God's miracle that brought us together."

And that is our story of Margaret and Ruth,who now call themselves Ebony and Ivory.

Margaret Patrick

优雅的黑色手指,另一只则具有短壮丰满的白色手指——有节奏地在黑白键上跳跃着。从那天起,她们几百次地一起坐在键盘前,玛格丽特残疾的右手搂着罗斯的后背,露思残疾的左手放在玛格丽特的膝上。露思健全的手弹着乐曲的旋律,而玛格丽特的好手弹着伴音。

她们的音乐受到电视观众的喜爱,在教堂、学校、康复处及城市中心受到普遍欢迎。在琴凳上,她们分享了除了音乐之外的许多东西。在那里,伴随着肖邦、巴赫、贝多芬的音乐,她们发现她们有许多做梦也想不到的共同之处。她们都是曾祖母,丈夫都过世了(玛格丽特的丈夫1985年去世),都失去过儿子,都想做些事情,但如果没有对方,她们什么也做不了。

坐在同一张琴凳上,露思听到玛格丽特说:"我的音乐被拿走了,但上帝给了我露思。"很显然在她们肩并肩共同度过的5年中,玛格丽特的想法和露思一样。露思现在这样说:"上帝创造了奇迹,它把我们带到一起。"

这就是我们的玛格丽特和露思的故事。她们现在把自己叫做"黑白琴键"。

玛格丽特·帕特里克

Make a Wish

I'll never forget the day Momma *made* me go to a birthday party.I was in Mrs.Black's third grade class in Wichita Falls,Texas,and I brought home a slightly peanut-buttery invitation.

"I'm not going," I said."She's a new girl named Ruth,and Berniece and Pat aren't going.She asked the whole class,all 36 of us."

As Momma studied the handmade invitation,she looked strangely sad.Then she announced,"Well,you are going! I'll pick up a present tomorrow."

I couldn't believe it.Momma had never made me go to a party! I was positive I'd just die if I had to go.But no amount of hysterics could sway Momma.

When Saturday arrived,Momma rushed me out of bed and made me wrap the pretty pink pearlized mirror-brush-and-comb set she'd bought for $2.98.

She drove me over in her yellow and white 1950 Oldsmobile.Ruth answered the door and motioned me to follow her up the steepest,scariest staircase I'd ever seen.

Stepping through the door brought great relief.The hardwood floors gleamed in the sun-filled parlor.Snow-white doilies covered the backs and arms of well-worn overstuffed furniture.

The biggest cake I ever saw sat on one table.It was decorated with nine pink candles,a messily printed Happy Birthday Ruthey and what I think were supposed to be rosebuds.

Thirty-six Dixie cups filled with homemade fudge were near the cake—each one with a name on it.

双语精华版·心灵鸡汤·

许愿

我永远忘不了那一天妈妈带我去参加一个生日派对。当时我在德克萨斯州位于维赤塔瀑布的学校布莱克夫人的三年级班上学,那天我带回一张沾了一点花生酱的生日派对请帖。

"我不去,"我说:"她是我们班新来的女孩,叫露思。伯尼和柏特都不去,她邀请了我们班所有的36个人。"

妈妈看着那张手工制作的邀请函,不知怎的她看起来有点难过。然后她宣布:"明天,你要去,我要给你准备一些礼物。"

我简直不敢相信。妈妈从来不让我参加派对,我敢肯定如果我一定要去,那我一定会死。然而这次不管我怎么闹,妈妈都不让步。

星期六到了,妈妈一早把我叫起来,让我穿上她花了2.98美元买来的漂亮的粉红色套装,上面带有闪着珍珠般光泽的镜子和小梳子图案。

她开着我们的黄白相间的1950年的老车。露思给我开门,带着我走上摇动得让人害怕的楼梯。

进入房间的门我才轻松下来,客厅的硬木地板在阳光下闪着光,铺着厚厚的软垫的旧家具靠背和扶手上罩着雪白的装饰巾。

一张桌子上放着我从没见过的巨大蛋糕,上面装饰着9支蜡烛,写着"露思,生日快乐!"几个歪歪斜斜的字还有一些像花蕾样的花纹。

蛋糕的旁边放着36只装着自制软糖的纸杯,上面都写了名字。

This won't be too awful—once everyone gets here,I decided.

"Where's your mom?" I asked Ruth.

Looking down at the floor,she said,"Well she's sorta sick."

"Oh.Where's your dad?"

"He's gone."

Then there was a silence,except for a few raspy coughs from be-hind a closed door.Some 15 minutes passed···then 10 more.Suddenly the terrifying realization set in.*No one else was coming.*How could I get out of here?As I sank into self-pity,I heard muffled sobs.Looking up I saw Ruth's tear-streaked face.All at once my eight-year-old heart was over-whelmed with sympathy for Ruth and filled with rage at my 35 selfish classmates.

Springing to my white-patent leather feet,I proclaimed at the top of my lungs,"Who needs 'em?"

Ruth's startled look changed to excited agreement.

There we were—two small girls and a triple-decker cake,36 candy-filled Dixie cups,ice cream,gallons of red Kool-Aid,three dozen party favors,games to play and prizes to win.

We started with the cake.We couldn't find any matches,and Ruthey (she was no longer just plain Ruth) wouldn't disturb her mom,so we just pretended to light them.I sang "Happy Birthday" while Ruthey made a wish and blew out the imaginary flames.

In a flash it was noon.Momma was honking out front.Gathering up all my goodies and thanking Ruthey repeatedly,I dashed to the car.I was bubbling over.

"I won *all* the games! Well,really,Ruthey won Pin the Tail on the Donkey,but she said it wasn't fair for the birthday girl to win a prize,so she gave it to me,and we split the party favors 50/50.Momma,she just loved the mirror set.I was the only one there—out of Mrs.Black's whole third-grade class.And I can't wait to tell every one of them what a great

我确定这些不会让人感觉太寒酸。

"你妈妈呢？"我问。

她低头看着地板说："她病了。"

"那你爸爸呢？"

"他走了。"

我们都不说话了，除了从一扇关着的门内传出几声尖锐的咳嗽声外，一片寂静。15分钟过去了，又过了10分钟，可怕的事情出现了，没有一个人到来。我该怎么办，觉得自己很无助，我听到压抑的哭声，抬头看到露思泪眼朦胧的脸。此时我只有8岁的心脏由于对露思的同情被压垮了，我痛恨那35个自私自利的同学。

我狠狠地跺着我白皮肤的脚，声嘶力竭地喊道："谁要他们？"

露思的脸色从震惊转变成激动的赞同。

我们，两个小女孩，一个3层的蛋糕，36个装着糖果的纸杯，冰淇淋，几加仑红色自制冷饮，3打给游戏获胜者的礼物，一起开始了派对。

我们从蛋糕开始，找不到火柴，露思（她不再是那个不起眼的露思）不想打扰她妈妈，所以我们假装点亮蜡烛，我唱着"生日快乐"歌，露思许了愿，吹灭了假想的火苗。

一眨眼到了中午，妈妈在外面喊我。收拾起所有的感伤，我再三向露思道谢，冲向汽车时我非常激动。

我赢了所有游戏，其实露思赢了给驴子贴尾巴的游戏，但她说过生日的孩子赢奖不公平所以让给了我。我们各人分了一半游戏奖品，妈妈只喜欢发光的东西，那天我是布莱尔夫人整个三年级唯一的一个，我忍不住要告诉所有的人他们错过了一个多么了不起的生

party they missed! "

Momma pulled over to the curb,stopped the car and hugged me tight.With tears in her eyes,she said,"I'm so proud of you! "

That was the day I learned that one person could really make a difference.I had made a big difference in Ruthey's ninth birthday,and Momma had made a big difference in my life.

LeAnne Reaves

日派对。

妈妈把车开到路边停下，紧紧地抱着我，含着热泪对我说："你是我的骄傲！"

就是那一天我知道了一个人可以创造奇迹。我为露思的9岁生日创造了奇迹。妈妈为我的人生创造了奇迹。

乐安妮·里维斯

ZIGGY© ZIGGY AND FRIENDS, INC. *Reprinted with permission of Universal Press Syndicate. All rights reserved.*

经典系列／光阴的故事

I Promise,Mama

CHICKEN
SOUP

A promise made is a debt unpaid.

Robert W.Service

"Jean Oliver Dyer," a voice said,and Jean crossed the stage,her head held high,her gown rippling in the breeze.

Suddenly,Jean's eyes fluttered open.Groggily,she wiped the sleep away and sighed.No graduation.No diploma.It was just a dream—a dream that won't come true,Jean thought sadly—and a promise I can't keep.I'm so sorry,Mama! She cried.

Growing up in Richmond,Virginia,Jean could read by age four. Whenever she asked for help with her homework,her mom,Amanda,said, "You're so smart you can do it yourself! "

Jean was smart enough to skip a grade—and to know how hard her mom worked.Amanda,who had left school to help support her family, now washed dishes to make a living."But someday," she'd tell Jean, "you're going to college."

The night Jean started the tenth grade,she found a new sweater and skirt on her bed.They're lovely! she thought,But Mama must have spent a month of paychecks on these! Her face burned.Mama shouldn't work so hard,she thought.I love school—but Mama needs me more.Soon,she dropped out,too. Disappointed tears shone in Amanda's eyes.

But it's for the best,Jean reminded herself.She found work at fast-food eateries and laundromats.One day,a young man with a shy smile asked her out.Almost before she knew it,they were married.

我答应你，妈妈

一个许下的承诺是一笔未偿还的债。

罗伯特·W. 瑟维斯

"珍妮·奥利弗·戴尔，"一个声音说道，珍妮穿过典礼台，高昂着头，毕业礼服在风中飘动。

突然，眼睛睁开了。珍妮揉着惺忪的睡眼，赶走睡意，深深叹了口气。没有毕业，没有文凭。这只是一个梦，永远不会实现的梦。珍妮悲伤地想，一个永远无法兑现的诺言。对不起，妈妈！珍妮伤心地哭了。

珍妮在弗尼吉亚的里士满长大，4岁就识字。每当求妈妈阿曼达帮助做作业时，妈妈就会说："你这么聪明，可以自己做。"

珍妮很聪明，在学校跳了级，在家里开始懂得了妈妈工作的艰辛。妈妈阿曼达为了养家，辍学回家，现在靠洗碗谋生。"终有一天，"她对珍妮讲，"你要上大学。"

珍妮十年级开学的头天晚上，发现床上有一件新外套和裙子。真漂亮！她想。为了买它们，妈妈肯定花光一个月的薪水！她的脸发烫。妈妈不该这么劳累。我爱学校，但妈妈更需要我。不久，她也退学了。失望的泪水在阿曼达的眼中闪耀着。

我这么做完全是好意，珍妮提醒自己。她在快餐厅和自助洗衣店里找到了工作。一天，一位笑容羞涩的年轻人邀请她出去。懵懵懂懂中，他们结了婚。

Jean became a mom—six times in seven years.Between sewing and washing sticky hands,she worked as a teacher's aide.But money was tight.I'd earn more if I had my diploma,she thought.

So Jean went to night school."Mommy has to go to school now," she'd laugh,kissing six little faces and racing off.

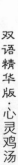

When Jean earned her GED at twenty-eight,her mom was ecstatic. "I knew you could do it! " she cried.

Jean enrolled in Virginia Commonwealth University for one class— and earned an A.

"That's my girl! " Amanda cried.

But as Jean began her second term,it was hard to stay focused.Does Ervin need help with fractions?she'd wonder.Did Dana take her bath?

"It's too much," Jean cried."My children need me." She was able to find a job as a supervisor at the housing authority,and she encouraged her kids to study hard."Mama," she'd boast,"all the children are on the honor roll! "

"When are you going to school?" Amanda would ask.Why is that so important?Jean fumed inside.I'm a hard worker,a good mother—why isn't that enough?But soon after her kids began heading to college, Jean's marriage crumbled.One day,she found herself alone,staring at a wall of job commendations.There was one vacant area—a spot for a college degree.

"Mama," she told Amanda,"I'm going back to school."

"I'm so happy! ' Amanda cried.

But it was hard.Jean needed three jobs to pay her bills and tuition. She often fell asleep over her books.That semester,she stared in shame at a row of Fs.

"It'll get better," Amanda encouraged."I'll help however I can."

Amanda's persistence—nagging,even—perplexed Jean.I was doing all right without a college degree,she'd think.So why…?

珍妮做了母亲，7年内生了6个孩子。在用粗糙的双手做家务活的间隙，还担任助教。可是，仍感到钱很紧张。她想，有了文凭，就会挣更多的钱。

珍妮28岁时，得到了高中同等学力，妈妈喜极而泣："我就知道你能做到的。"

珍妮在弗尼吉亚联邦大学注册了一门课，获得了A的成绩。"这才是我姑娘呢！"阿曼达高声地说。

第2学期开始了，但珍妮很难集中精力，她会想：埃文需要帮助讲解分数吗？达娜洗澡了吗？

"够了，"珍妮哭道，"孩子们需要我。"于是，她找到了一个房产管理员的工作。她积极鼓励孩子们努力学习。"妈妈，"她骄傲地说。"所有的孩子都上了光荣榜！"

每当这时，阿曼达就会问："你什么时候上学？"上学这么重要吗？珍妮暗自懊恼。我是一个工作努力的人，一个好妈妈，还不够吗？

不久，孩子们开始上大学了，珍妮的婚姻却解体了。一天，她独自凝视着满墙的工作嘉奖状，还缺一个——大学学位。

"妈妈，"她告诉阿曼达，"我要回到学校去。"

"太好了！"阿曼达叫道。

说起来容易，做起来难。珍妮需要做3份工作才能支付账单和学费。她经常捧着书本睡着了。那学期，她羞愧地面对一排的F(不及格)。

"会好起来的，"阿曼达鼓励她，"我会尽可能地帮助你。"

阿曼达对大学的执著，困扰着珍妮，让她迷茫。没有大学学历，我一切也都不错。那么为什么……？

One day,she got her answer.Amanda had been offered a post on the church council—and she'd turned it down.

"Why?" Jean cried.

Amanda looked down at her feet. "There's so much paperwork to do," she blurted. "And I···I can't read! "

The words felt like a slap to Jean.How could I not have known?she wondered.She thought back to how,as a child,she'd had to read recipes aloud,how Amanda wouldn't help with her homework.That's why it matters so much to her for me to achieve! she realized.

"Oh,I'll teach you to read,Mama! " Jean cried.

But Jean didn't have that chance.Soon after,Amanda was diagnosed with a brain tumor.

I can't bear to lose her! Jean wept.She tiptoed into Amanda's room, where her mom reached out a hand.

"What is it,Mama?" Jean asked.

"Promise one thing," Amanda murmured. "Promise me you'll finish college."

Jean bit her lip.This had been her dream for so long.How can I not?"I promise,Mama," she whispered.

From then on,Jean threw herself into her studies,rushing to Amanda's side after class. "I'm here,Mama," she'd say softly.

"You should be studying! " Amanda would scold.

When Amanda slipped away,Jean felt hollow with grief. There was only one thing to do:keep her promise.

Then one day,Jean awoke with chest pains and needed surgery for a heart problem.And now,as she recovered at home,she worried she'd never make Amanda's dream come true.I've failed you,Mama,she wept. I'll never graduate!

All of a sudden,she could swear she heard a familiar voice. "Yes," it urged. "Yes,you will."

一天,她得到了答案。有人给阿曼达提供了一份教会委员会的岗位,但是她拒绝了。

阿曼达低头看着脚。"有很多的书面工作要做,"她吞吞吐吐地说,"我,我不识字。"

这些话像鞭子一样抽打着珍妮。我怎么会不知道呢?她明白过来,想起过去孩子时,她要大声地读食谱给阿曼达,阿曼达还不能帮助她做作业。原因就在这儿,所以才让阿曼达意识到让我获得学历是多么重要!

"噢,妈妈,我教你识字!"珍妮说道。

但是,珍妮没有机会了。不久,阿曼达被诊断得了脑瘤。

我不能忍受失去她的痛苦!珍妮哭泣着。她蹑手蹑脚地走进阿曼达的房间,阿曼达伸出了一只手。

"妈妈,什么事?"珍妮问道。

"答应我一件事,"阿曼达喃喃地说,"答应我一定读完大学。"

珍妮咬紧嘴唇。这是她多年的梦想。我怎么会不呢?"我答应你,妈妈。"她低声答道。

从此以后,珍妮全部精力都投入到学习中。放学后,就冲到阿曼达的旁边。"我来了,妈妈,"她轻声地说。

"你该学习呀。"阿曼达会责怪道。

阿曼达去世了,珍妮被痛苦掏空了身子。还有一件事情可做:履行诺言。

一天,珍妮被胸痛弄醒,她的心脏出了问题,需要做手术。在家休养时,她担心永远不会实现阿曼达的梦想。妈妈,我让你失望了,她哭道。我永远不会毕业。

突然,她确信听到了一个熟悉的声音。"不,"这个声音坚决地说,"不,你一定会毕业的。"

"You're right,Mama," she whispered. "You've always been right."

Soon,Jean was back on her feet—and back in school.On her lunch hour at work as an investigator for the police department,she'd read textbooks,then stay up late into the night writing papers.

And on Mother's Day 1996,as Jean slipped her graduation gown on,she felt a rush of pride.I kept my promise,Mama,she thought.How I wish you could see me now!

As she crossed the Saint Paul's College stage to accept her bachelor's degree and her grandchildren cheered,"Way to go,Granny! " Jean looked heavenward.You do see me,Mama,don't you?She smiled.

Today,Jean,fifty-eight,is one course away from her master's degree, and she's establishing a parenting program for low-income moms. "I want to be a source of strength for them,like my mom was for me," she says.

Each night as she studies,she gazes proudly at her diploma on the wall.But her real inspiration comes from the photo on the table—the one of Amanda smiling.I finally did it,Mama,Jean thinks.For me—and for you.

Jean Oliver Dyer

Excerpted from **Woman's World**

很快，珍妮可以下地走路了，回到了学校。当政府部门调查员的午休时间，她要读书，晚上熬夜写作业。

1996年的母亲节，珍妮穿上了毕业礼服，感到由衷骄傲。我遵守了诺言，妈妈，她想。我多么希望你现在能看见我呀！

当她走上圣保罗大学的典礼台，接过学士学位证书时，孙子们高声喝彩："奶奶，你真行！"珍妮向天望去。你看见我了，妈妈，对吗？珍妮笑了。

今天，珍妮58岁了，还有一科就硕士毕业了。她为低收入母亲们建立一个资助项目。"我想成为她们力量的源泉，就像妈妈对我那样。"她说。

每到晚上学习时，珍妮就骄傲地凝视着墙上的证书。但她真正的灵感来自桌上——阿曼达微笑的照片。珍妮想，妈妈，我做到了，为我，也为你。

珍妮·奥利弗·戴尔
摘自《女性世界》

The Dolphin's Gift

CHICKEN SOUP

I was in about 40 feet of water, alone. I knew I should not have gone alone,but I was very competent and just took a chance. There was not much current,and the water was so warm, clear and enticing. When I got a cramp, I realized at once how foolish I was. I was not too alarmed, but *was* completely doubled up with stomach cramps.I tried to remove my weight belt,but I was so doubled up I could not get to the catch.I was sinking and began to feel more frightened,unable to move.I could see my watch and knew there was only a little more time on the tank before I would be out of air. I tried to massage my abdomen. I wasn't wearing a wet suit, but couldn't straighten out and couldn't get to the cramped muscles with my hands.

I thought,"I can't go like this! I have things to do!"I just couldn't die anonymously this way with no one to even know what happened to me. I called out in my mind,"Somebody, something, help me! "

I was not prepared for what happened.Suddenly I felt a prodding from behind me under the armpit. I thought, "Oh no, sharks! "I felt real terror and despair. But my arm was being lifted forcibly. Around into my field of vision came an eye—the most marvelous eye I could ever imagine. I swear it was smiling. It was the eye of a big dolphin. Looking into that eye, I knew I was safe.

It moved farther forward, nudging under and hooking its dorsal fin below my armpit with my arm over its back. I relaxed, hugging it, flooded with relief. I felt that the animal was conveying security to me, that it was healing me as well as lifting me toward the surface. My stomach cramps went away as we ascended and I relaxed with security,

双语精华版·心灵鸡汤·

海豚的礼物

　　我,独自一人,正待在40英尺深的水下。知道本不该一个人去,但因为水性不错,我就冒了一次险。水流不急,缓和,清澈,诱人。只是胃部痉挛的时候,才意识到自己是多么愚蠢。我并不害怕,但胃痉挛痛得直不起腰。我试图拿掉腰上的加重带,但因身体弯曲,够不到锁扣。身体开始下沉,越发害怕起来,浑身僵硬。看到表上的时间,知道用不了多少时间氧气瓶就会用光。我竭力想去按摩胃部,但因为穿的不是湿式潜水服,身体挺不直,手够不到痉挛的肌肉部分。

　　我心想:"不能就这么完了!一定要做些什么!"不能以这种方式默默无闻地死去。我心中大声呼唤:"快救救我!"

　　接下来发生的事情让我始料未及。突然觉得腋窝有什么东西从背后顶来。"哦,不,是鲨鱼!"我感到真正的恐惧和绝望。但是胳臂被有力地抬了起来,在视力所及的范围内看见了一只所能想象的最奇妙的眼睛,我敢肯定她在笑。这是一只大海豚的眼睛,凝望着那只眼睛,我知道得救了。

　　海豚向前方游去,我用手搂着她的背,在我的腋窝下她用背鳍钩着我,轻轻地推着走。抱着海豚,我身心舒缓,轻松自在,觉得这只动物正给我送来安全,正给我治疗,正把我运上水面。上来时,胃痉挛消失了,虽然有安全登陆、身体放松的原因,但我坚持认为是海豚

but I felt very strongly that it healed me too.

At the surface it drew me all the way into shore. It took me into water so shallow that I began to be concerned that it might be beached, and I pushed it back a little deeper, where it waited, watching me, I guess to see if I was all right.

It felt like another lifetime. When I took off the weight belt and oxygen tank, I just took everything off and went naked back into the ocean to the dolphin. I felt so light and free and alive, and just wanted to play in the sun and the water in all that freedom. The dolphin took me back out and played around in the water with me. I noticed that there were a lot of dolphins there, farther out.

After a while it brought me back to shore. I was very tired then, almost collapsing and he made sure I was safe in the shallowest water. Then he turned sideways with one eye looking into mine. We stayed that way for what seemed like a very long time, timeless I guess, in a trance almost, with personal thoughts from the past going through my mind. Then he made just one sound and went out to join the others. And all of them left.

Elizabeth Gawain

治愈了我。

　　海豚一直在水面上拖我到岸边,把我送到浅水区,我担心她会搁浅,把她推回到深一些的水域。她等在那里,看着我,猜她是要看我安全到岸。

　　这像又一次的生命轮回。脱下加重带,脱下氧气瓶,脱下所有的负重,赤身回到海洋,回到海豚身边,我感到轻松、自由和快乐,只想在这自由之中,在阳光下,在海水中尽情地玩耍。海豚把我带回海中,然后在我身旁戏水。我发现,在远处,还有很多海豚。

　　过了一会儿,她把我送回岸边。我当时很累,摇摇晃晃。海豚确定我到了最浅的安全水域后,才侧转过身,一只眼睛凝望着我。就这样凝望着我,仿佛过了很长时间,我想是永远。刚发生的一幕幕恍恍惚惚地在脑海中又一次闪现,让我感慨万千。接着,海豚一声呼啸,游回到伙伴的身边,一起离开。

伊丽莎白·高文

The Cowboy's Story

CHICKEN SOUP

When I started my telecommunications company, I knew I was going to need salespeople to help me expand the business. I put the word out that I was looking for qualified salespeople and began the interviewing process. The salesperson I had in mind was experienced in the telemarketing communications industry, knew the local market, had experience with the various types of systems available, had a professional demeanor and was a self-starter. I had very little time to train a person, so it was important that the salesperson I hired could "hit the ground running."

During the tiresome process of interviewing prospective salespeople, into my office walked a cowboy. I knew he was a cowboy by the way he was dressed. He had on corduroy pants and a corduroy jacket that didn't match the pants; a short-sleeved snap-button shirt; a tie that came about halfway down his chest with a knot bigger than my fist; cowboy boots; and a baseball cap. You can imagine what I was thinking: "Not what I had in mind for my new company." He sat down in front of my desk, took off his cap and said, "Mister, I'd just shore appreciate a chance to be a success in the telephone biness." And that's just how he said it, too: biness.

I was trying to figure out a way to tell this fellow, without being too blunt, that he just wasn't what I had in mind at all. I asked him about his background. He said he had a degree in agriculture from Oklahoma

牛仔传奇

我的通信公司刚刚起步,需要销售人员拓展业务。我传出话去,说要雇佣合格的销售人员,然后就开始面试。心目中合格的销售人员的标准:在远程通信营销行业有过工作经验的,了解当地的市场,熟悉各种通信系统,有职业道德,白手起家。我没有时间培训,所以雇佣的这个销售员要尽快进入角色。

对有希望的应试人员进行面试很枯燥。有一天,走进一个牛仔,他的穿着让我得出一个判断。他穿着灯芯绒短裤,配着极不协调的灯芯绒夹克,套着短袖按扣衬衫,领带结比拳头还大,半耷拉在胸前,蹬着牛仔靴,戴着垒球帽。你肯定知道我会想什么:"这绝不是我想象中公司的人。"他坐在我的桌子前,摘下垒球帽说:"先生,我真是很高兴能有机会体验电话生业的成功。"他就是这么说的:生业。

我试图想出一种比较委婉的方式告诉他,他根本不是我想要的人,于是就问了他的一些背景情况。他说在俄克拉何马州立大学获得了学位。在过去的5年中,每个夏天都在该州的巴特斯维尔牧场打

State University and that he had been a ranch hand in Bartlesville, Oklahoma, for the past few years during the summers. He announced that was all over now, he was ready to be a success in "biness," and he would just "shore appreciate a chance."

We continued to talk. He was so focused on success and how he would "shore appreciate a chance" that I decided to give him a chance. I told him that I would spend two days with him. In those two days I would teach him everything I thought he needed to know to sell one type of very small telephone system. At the end of those two days he would be on his own. He asked me how much money I thought he could make.

I told him, "Looking like you look and knowing what you know, the best you can do is about $1,000 per month." I went on to explain that the average commission on the small telephone systems he would be selling was approximately $250 per system. I told him if he would see 100 prospects per month, that he would sell four of those prospects a telephone system. Selling four telephone systems would give him $1,000. I hired him on straight commission with no base salary.

He said that sounded great to him because the most he had ever made was $400 per month as a ranch hand and he was ready to make some money. The next morning, I sat him down to cram as much of the telephone "biness" I could into a 22-year-old cowboy with no business experience, no telephone experience and no sales experience. He looked like anything but a professional salesperson in the telecommunications business. In fact, he had none of the qualities I was looking for in an employee, except one: He had an incredible focus on being a success.

At the end of two days of training, Cowboy (that's what I called him then, and still do) went to his cubicle. He took out a sheet of paper and wrote down four things:

工。他声明现在一切都结束了,准备在"生业"上取得成功,他"真是很高兴能有机会"。

我们继续交谈。他非常关注成功,而且"真是很高兴能有机会",我决定给他这个机会。我告诉他,给他两天时间。在这两天里,我教他销售小型电话系统需要掌握的内容。第2天结束,他就自己单干。他问我认为他能挣多少钱。

我告诉他:"凭你的外表和知识水平,你最多每月挣1000美元。"我接着解释道, 他要卖的这种小型通话系统的平均佣金是每套250美元。如果每月能见100个有意向的客户,会卖出4个。卖4个会得到1000美元。我雇佣他,给的全是佣金,没有底薪。

他说,听起来不错。他挣得最多的是在农场干活,每月400美元。他已经做好了挣钱的准备。第2天一早,我就尽我所能向这个没有任何商业经验,没有任何电信经验,没有任何销售经验的22岁牛仔灌输电信"生业"知识。他根本就不像通讯行业的专业人士。事实上,他不具备任何我所预期的职员应有的品质。唯一可取之处就是:对成功有令人难以置信的关注。

两天培训之后,牛仔(我当时这么称呼他,现在仍然这么称呼他)走进他的小房间,取出一张纸,写下了4句话:

1.I will be a success in business.

2.I will see 100 people per month.

3.I will sell four telephone systems per month.

4.I will make $1,000 per month.

He placed this sheet of paper on the cubicle wall in front of him and started to work.

At the end of the first month,he hadn't sold four telephone systems.However,at the end of his first ten days,he had sold seven telephone systems.

At the end of his first year,Cowboy hadn't earned $12,000 in commissions.Instead,he had earned over $60,000 in commissions.

He was indeed amazing.One day,he walked into my office with a contract and payment on a telephone system.I asked him how he had sold this one.He said,"I just told her, 'Ma'am,if it don't do nothing but ring and you answer it,it's a heck of a lot prettier than that one you got. 'She bought it."

The woman wrote him a check in full for the telephone system,but Cowboy wasn't really sure I would take a check,so he drove her to the bank and had her get cash to pay for the system.He carried thousand dollar bills into my office and said,"Larry,did I do good? " I assured him that he did good!

After three years,he owned half of my company.At the end of another year,he owned three other companies.At that time we separated as business partners.He was driving a $32,000 black pickup truck.He was wearing $600 cowboy-cut suits,$500 cowboy boots and a three-carat horseshoe-shaped diamond ring.He had become a success in"biness."

What made Cowboy a success? Was it because he was a hard

1. 做买卖一定成功。

2.每个月要见100位顾客。

3.每个月卖4台通信系统。

4.每个月挣1000美元。

他把这张纸贴在了卧室的墙上，开始工作。

第1个月，他不是卖4台通信系统，而是10天就卖了7台通信系统。

第1年，他不是挣12,000美元的佣金，而是挣了60,000美元。

这个牛仔真神奇。一天，他走进我的办公室，带着一份通讯系统的销售合同和货款。我问他怎么卖出去的，他说：“我只是告诉她：‘夫人，就算它只能当铃用，你接电话时听到的声音也要比你现在的电话强10,000倍。’于是，她就买下了。”

3年过后，他拥有了我公司的一半股份。第4年底，他拥有了其他3家公司。同年，我们分开发展。他开上了一辆32,000美元的黑色皮卡车，身穿600美元的牛仔夹克，脚蹬500美元的牛仔靴，戴着一个3克拉鞋型的钻石项链。他在“生业”上成功了。

是什么让牛仔成功了？就因为他工作努力吗？这些因素起了一

worker? That helped. Was it because he was smarter than everyone else? No. He knew nothing about the telephone business when he started. So what was it? I believe it was because he knew the Ya Gotta's for Success:

He was focused on success. He knew that's what he wanted and he went after it.

He took responsibility. He took responsibility for where he was, who he was and what he was (a ranch hand). Then he took action to make it different.

He made a decision to leave the ranch in Bartlesville, Oklahoma, and to look for opportunities to become a success.

He changed. There was no way that he could keep doing the things that he had been doing and receive different results. And he was willing to do what was necessary to make success happen for him.

He had vision and goals. He saw himself as a success. He also had written down specific goals. He wrote down the four items that he intended to accomplish and put them on the wall in front of him. He saw those goals every day and focused on their accomplishment.

He put action to his goals and stayed with it even when it got tough. It wasn't always easy for him. He experienced slumps like everyone does. He got more doors slammed in his face and telephones in his ear than any salesperson I have ever known. But he never let it stop him. He kept on going.

He asked. Boy, did he ask! First he asked me for a chance, then he asked nearly all the people he came across if they wanted to buy a telephone system from him. And his asking paid off. As he likes to put it, "Even a blind hog finds an acorn every once in a while." That simply means that if you ask enough, eventually someone will say yes.

些作用。是因为他比其他人聪明吗？不。开始创业时，他对通讯行业一无所知。那么，因为什么呢？我认为，这是因为他知道"成功的要诀"：

他关注成功，知道成功是他的追求。

他承担责任，敢于正视自己的地位、身份和职业（一个农场的雇工），然后采取行动，改变现状。

他决心离开俄克拉何马州的巴特斯维尔牧场，寻找机会，取得成功。

他勇于改变。如果一成不变的话，结果将会大相径庭。他愿意为成功做任何必需的事情。

他有远见和目标。他预见到自己的成功，写下具体的目标。他在自己房间的墙上写下4个具体要完成的任务，每天都浏览这些任务，然后一心一意地完成它们。

他不畏艰难，为实现目标付出行动。对他而言，事情并非一帆风顺。像其他人一样，他体验到生意的萧条。他吃的闭门羹决不比我所知的任何一个销售员少。但是，这没有阻止他，他一如既往。

他勤学好问。真的，他确实很好问！他先从我这儿问出了一个机会。然后，几乎问遍所有遇到的人是否愿意买电话系统。接着，得到了回报。正如他喜欢说的那样："即使是一头瞎眼猪早晚也能撞见榫果。"道理很简单，如果你问得勤，总会有人说"好的"。

He cared. He cared about me and his customers. He discovered that when he cared more about taking care of his customers than he cared about taking care of himself, it wasn't long before he didn't have to worry about taking care of himself.

Most of all, Cowboy started every day as a winner! He hit the front door expecting something good to happen. He believed that things were going to go his way regardless of what happened. He had no expectation of failure, only an expectation of success. And I've found that when you expect success and take action on that expectation, you almost always get success.

Cowboy has made millions of dollars. He has also lost it all, only to get it all back again. In his life as in mine, it has been that once you know and practice the principles of success, they will work for you again and again.

He can also be an inspiration to you. He is proof that it's not environment or education or technical skills and ability that make you a success. He proves that it takes more: It takes the principles we so often overlook or take for granted. These are the principles of the Ya Gotta's for Success.

Larry Winget

他关心人，关心我和客户。他发现，如果他关心客户多于关心自己，用不了多久，他就不必再关心自己了。

最重要的，牛仔每天都以胜利者的姿态开始。从打开房门起就期望一切顺利，相信不管发生了什么事，自己总会如意。他没有想到失败，只期望成功。我发现，如果人们期望成功，并为之付诸行动，多半会成功的。

牛仔成了百万富翁。他也曾经马失前蹄，却又东山再起。在他和我的一生中都是如此：一旦知道成功的道理，并为之奋斗，这些道理就会一而再，再而三地得到应验。

牛仔对大家也是一种激励。他证明，并不是环境、教育、技能或者能力使你成功。他证明，成功不只需要这些，还需要撇开那些理所当然的道理。这就是"成功的要决"。

拉里·温格特

经典系列／光阴的故事

Perfectly Normal

The year was 1963.

That's when I was born...to "perfectly normal" parents at a "perfectly normal" Cleveland hospital.

I would like to say that I was a "perfectly normal", healthy baby, ready to take on the world.But instead,I was born with multiple deformities.My eyes were almost on the sides of my head,and I only had holes where my nose was supposed to be.I had a club foot and was missing all but one toe,if it could be called that.Also,three of my fingers were missing on my right hand.A cleft palate had an opening in my top lip and extended all the way to the right eye.Unfortunately,even one leg was shorter than the other.

The hospital staff,I was told,thought I had too many problems to survive.The doctors,in fact,refused to show me to my parents and, incredulously,even gave my parents forms to sign to "give me up for science".

I can only thank God that my parents had other plans for my life.I belonged to them and to God.They intended to love and accept me just as I was,despite acknowledging that it would be a long,hard road ahead.

At the age of seven months,I began to undergo a very long series of operations.However,the first seven were deemed failures.The surgeons,it seemed were trying to do too much at once.I,on the other hand, was like a puzzle that needed to be "put together" one piece at a time.

完全正常

那是1963年。

那年我那"完全正常"的父母在"完全正常"的克里夫兰医院给了我生命。

很想说我是一个"完全正常"、健康的孩子,正准备迎接世界。可是,我却有很多先天缺陷。眼睛几乎都挪到了脸一边,所谓的鼻子不过是两个洞,脚也畸形,只有一个脚趾,如果那可以称为脚趾的话。另外,右手缺3根手指,兔唇的裂口一直延伸到右眼睛。双腿健全,可不幸的是一条腿长,一条腿短。

据说,医务人员认为我太"健全"了,存活的希望不大。事实上,医生拒绝把我送给父母看。更难以置信的是,给他们表格,让他们写上"为科学而放弃。"

感谢上帝,父母对我另有安排。我属于他们,属于上帝。无论怎么样,他们打算接受我,尽管承认这将是一条长长的、充满艰辛之路。

7个月时,我开始经历一系列的手术。最初的7次手术都失败了。一方面,医生们似乎总想一次就解决所有的问题。另一方面,我就像一个智力拼图,一次只能拼上一块。

CHICKEN SOUP

While successive surgeries were a little more successful, my appearance was still far from normal. In fact, very few people knew that I had already had sixteen operations by the time I was ready for third grade.

When I began kindergarten, I was placed in a special-education classroom because my appearance and imperfect speech were not accepted. Aside from being labeled a "special-ed" kid, I endured constant ridicule from other students who called me "stupid", "ugly" and "retarded" because of my looks. I also walked with a limp and had to wear special shoes and braces on my legs. I spent almost every school holiday in the hospital having operations and also missed a lot of school. I wondered if I would ever get out of special classes. My desire to become a "normal" child prompted my parents to pursue tests that would place me back in regular education classrooms. My parents and I worked very hard that summer to get ready for the big test. Finally, I was tested.

I'll never forget the day I waited outside the principal's office while my parents received my test results. The brown door between them and me seemed to loom bigger and bigger as time went by. Time passed in slow motion. I longed to put my ear to the door to hear what was being said.

After an hour passed, my mother finally emerged with a tear streaming down her cheek. I thought, oh, no, another year in special-ed. But much to my relief, the principal put his hand on my shoulder and said, "Welcome to 3B, young man! " My mom gave me a big hug.

Another milestone in fourth grade was the "miracle" that my parents and I had longed for. I was selected to undergo a very experimental surgery that would resculpt my entire face with bone grafts. The surgery was lifethreatening and lasted ten hours. I survived this operation, my

尽管接下来的手术成功一些,我的外表仍然距离正常很远。说真的,很少有人知道,到上三年级时,我已经做了16次手术了。

开始上幼儿园时,因为外表可怖,口齿不清,怕别人接受不了,我就被安排在一个接受特殊教育的教室。除了被认为是"特教生"外,因为外表,我还要忍受其他学生不断的嘲弄,他们称我为"蠢蛋"、"丑鬼"和"呆子"。走路一瘸一拐,要穿特制的鞋子,腿上绑着支架。几乎每次学校放假,都要上医院手术,也因此缺了很多课。不知道是否能走出"特教班"。想成为一个"正常"孩子的希望,促使父母不停地让我参加能回到普通班的测试。那年夏天,父母和我都尽了很大努力,准备一次重要的测试。最终,参加了测试。

永远也不会忘记那一天。父母去取测试结果,我等在校长办公室的外面。隔开父母和我的棕色的门,随着时间的逝去似乎越来越庞大。时间过得很慢,我急得把耳朵贴到门上,想知道他们在说什么。

一个小时过去了,妈妈终于出来了,一滴泪珠滑下她的面颊。噢,不,还得在特教班再呆一年,我想。但校长的话让我大松了一口气,他把手放在我的肩上,高兴地说:"年轻人,欢迎到3B班。"妈妈紧紧拥抱了我。

四年级是另一个里程碑,父母和我盼望已久的"奇迹"发生了。医生们挑选我进行一个实验性的手术,就是采用骨移植的方法重新造脸。这种手术有生命危险,持续了10个小时。终于,鼻子有形了,嘴

eighteenth,which really changed my life.At last,my nose had a shape,my lip was "fixed" and my eyes were very close to being in their normal position.

While I now faced a new chapter in my life from a physical perspective,I hadn't seen the end of my trials.

Within the next few years,my mother developed cancer and died, but not before instilling in me a sense of worth and the determination never to give up.

When other kids called me names,she had prompted, "Don't let those names bother you.Feel sorry for those kids who were not brought up right."

In addition,my parents taught me to be thankful for my blessings, pointing out that other people might have even greater challenges.

Their words eventually impacted my life when I did see people with greater challenges—in hospitals and whenever I did volunteer work with children who were mentally challenged.

As a teenager,I came to realize that my purpose in life was to help others become successful with whatever gifts they were blessed with,despite the things that society might point out as handicaps or shortcomings.In fact,my father advised, "Mike,you would make a great special-ed teacher." I knew what it was like to be a special-ed child.

However,I simply wasn't ready to make teaching my career choice at that point.Instead,I earned a degree in business and went on to become a very successful salesman,spending seven years in retail management.Then,I went on to become a very successful bank employee,spending five years as a loan officer. Still,something in my life was missing.

Despite the fact that I had met and married a specialed teacher,it took me twelve years to realize that was my calling also and that my dad had been right.

唇"补"全了，眼睛接近正常的位置了。

尽管从外表方面，生活展开了新篇章，可是仍没有看到磨难的尽头。

几年后，妈妈患癌症不幸去世了，但她却教会我认识自己的价值和永不放弃的决心。

其他孩子叫我绰号时，她激励我说："不要为那些绰号烦心。这些孩子缺少教养，你该为他们感到惋惜。"

父母还教我学会感激，指出其他人也许面临更大的挑战。

父母的谆谆教导一直影响我的生活。每当看见其他人面临更大的挑战时，在医院里，在我主动帮助那些大脑有缺陷的孩子时，我都会想起他们的教诲。

作为一个十几岁的孩子，我逐渐认识到，生活的目的就是帮助那些被赐予不同天赋的人们取得成功，也许世界会把他们的天赋称为残疾或者短处。爸爸建议说："麦克，你会成为一个伟大的特教教师的。"我知道一个特教孩子意味着什么。

然而，我没有准备好选择教师作为职业。我获得了一个商业方面的学位，接着成了一名成功的销售员，在零售业管理方面一干就是7年。后来，又成了一名非常成功的银行职工，做了5年信贷工作。生活中还是缺少些什么。

我遇到了一位特教教师，和她结了婚。可是足足花了12年的时间，我才意识到，这就是上帝对我的召唤，父亲说的话是对的。

Continuing my college education,pursuing a master's degree in education,I now teach in the same school district as my wife.

My classroom is a kaleidoscope of children with special needs—emotional,physical and mental.My newest career choice is my most challenging yet.I love to see my students' smiling faces when they learn something new,when a few words are spoken and when an award is won in the Special Olympics.

I've now gone through twenty-nine surgeries.While many have brought a lot of pain to my life,the fact that I have survived them all only seems to reiterate to me that God has a purpose for my life,as well as for every other life.I see my purpose being fulfilled one child at a time.

I may not have been a "perfectly normal" healthy baby,but I am ready to take on the world—thanks to God and to people like my mom. The motto she gave me will always be the motto I use in my own classroom:Never give up.

Michael Biasini

我上了大学，攻读教育学硕士学位。现在，我和妻子在同一学区教书。

课堂就像一个万花筒，各种各样有特殊需求的孩子层出不穷。这些需求有情感方面的，有身体方面的，有精神方面的。这一新选择的职业最富有挑战性。当学生们学到新东西时，当新词说出来时，当他们获得特奥会的奖章时，他们笑得那么灿烂。我喜欢看他们的笑脸。

现在，已经做过了29次手术了。多次手术给我的生活带来许多痛苦，但我却活了下去，这似乎一次又一次说明，上帝造我有特殊的目的，如同上帝造任何人都有其目的一样。每一次，在每一个孩子身上，我看见了我的目的实现。

我也许不是"完全正常"、健康的孩子，但我随时迎接世界。感谢上帝，感谢像妈妈那样的人，她赐给我课堂上永远的座右铭：永不放弃。

迈克尔·拜厄斯尼

经典系列／光阴的故事

Snowed In

Never doubt that a small group of thoughtful,committed people can change the world,indeed it's the only thing that ever has.

Margaret Mead

If it takes a village to raise a child,then January 17,1994,was the day it took a village to save a child.

Barbara Schmitt sipped coffee and watched the snow outside her window pile up.The city of Louisville,Kentucky,was paralyzed,with drifts up to two feet deep,but she and the two granddaughters she was helping to raise didn't mind.They were going to spend the day warm indoors,playing and watching the blizzard. Ashley,age six,chatted excitedly.Her three-year-old sister Michelle was subdued.Michelle was one of the hundreds of American children awaiting a new liver.

Waiting and praying were a daily routine for Barbara Schmitt,but today the prayers were more intense.Michelle had been showing danger signs that made an immediate liver transplant critical,but the telephone was as silent as the snowy scene outside.

Then at nine in the morning,the phone rang.Here was the news Barbara needed.A hospital in Omaha had located the right liver donor, they were sure it was a match for Michelle,and they needed her there within 12 hours.

Barbara couldn't tell what to do first—rejoice or despair.The greatest gift Michelle would ever receive was awaiting her,and here they were,snowbound,600 miles away. "We're snowed in," Barbara told the

雪花飘飘

　　永远不要怀疑人们想到的哪怕是很微小的办法，只要去行动，就能改变一切，事实就是这样的。

玛格瑞特·米德

　　如果需要整个村庄养育一个孩子的话，那么1994年1月17日，那一天整个村庄参与挽救一个孩子的生命。

　　芭芭拉·施密特一边喝着咖啡，一边观看着窗外堆积的大雪。肯塔基州路易维尔市的雪花堆积有两英尺深，城镇几乎瘫痪了。她和自己帮忙教养的两个孙女并不太担心，她们打算在温暖的房间里度过这一天，观赏大风雪还可以玩雪。6岁的爱西莉兴奋地夸夸其谈。而她3岁的妹妹米歇尔很安静，她是美国上千个等待捐肝的儿童之一。

　　等待和祈祷是芭芭拉·施密特每天必做的事，但是，今天祈祷更加虔诚。米歇尔已经有很危险的迹象，必须马上进行肝脏移植手术。但是，电话就像外面的雪景一样，安安静静，一直不响。

　　上午9点时，电话终于响了，传来了芭芭拉需要的消息。位于奥马哈的一家医院找到了合适的捐赠的肝脏。他们肯定各种指标与米歇尔相匹配。但是，他们要求一定要在12小时内到达他们医院。

　　芭芭拉起初不知该怎么办，又欣喜，又失望，给米歇尔的最大的礼物正在等着她，而她们这儿被大雪封住，离医院有600英里。芭芭拉对电话另一端的医院联系人说："我们这儿被雪封住了，机场在17

medical coordinator on the line. "The airport is 17 miles away, trucks are jackknifing off the roads, and there's no way we're going to get there."

"Don't give up," the woman told Barbara. "You have 12 hours to reach Omaha, so start thinking! "

Fortunately, the phone lines were still working, so Barbara got to work. She started by calling Sharon Stevens, a hairdresser who runs Hair Angels, a fund for children with special needs. Sharon had already lined up a Lear jet and two pilots to fly the Schmitts to Omaha when transplant time came. How to get from the Schmitts' house to the jet was the big question, but Sharon was as determined as Barbara to make this work. "Start packing. I don't know how, but you're going to make it."

Next, Sharon put out a call for help through the local radio station. WHAS broadcast continuous messages, inviting listeners to call in with ideas and suggestions. Teresa Amshoff heard the story and suggested that the church parking lot adjoining her house, only a mile from the Schmitts, would make a perfect helicopter landing pad. As precious minutes ticked away, the Amshoffs rushed from door to door, pleading for help to clear the lot. Neighbors, already exhausted from shoveling their own driveways, came without hesitation. Within half an hour, 50 volunteers were working in subzero winds to clear the area of snow.

Someone called Kim Phelps of Skycare, an airlift service, and he offered to dispatch a helicopter to take Michelle to the airport. The church lot was confirmed as a workable launch pad, and Kim got busy arranging rides to the church for the medical team.

In the meantime, Barbara called Lear jet pilot Jason Smith to be sure he could make it to the airport. Like everyone else, he and his co-pilot were snowbound, but he promised that they would be there. A policeman and neighbor were able to drive them to the jet just in time.

Finally, with dusk looming, WHAS sent a four-wheel vehicle to transport Michelle and her family to the church. When they pulled into

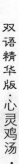

双语精华版·心灵鸡汤·

英里外,道路已被阻断,也没有其他的路可以到达那里。"

"不要放弃,"那位女士告诉芭芭拉:"到奥马哈之前,你们还有12小时,所以赶快开始想办法。"

幸运的是,电话线一直畅通。芭芭拉开始行动了。她打电话给莎伦·史蒂文斯,他是一名发型师,建立了救助儿童急需的救助基金——美发天使。莎伦还有一架理尔喷气飞机,两名飞行员,在运输繁忙的季节飞施密特至奥马哈航线。怎样才能从施密特家里去机场还是个大问题。但是莎伦和芭芭拉一样,下定决心一定要办到。"开始准备好要带的东西,虽然现在我不知道怎么办,但一定要办到。"

接着,莎伦给当地的无线广播电台打了求助电话,WHAS广播电台持续广播着这条消息征求听众的意见和建议。特蕾莎·安肖夫听到后,提出一个建议,与她住所毗连的一个教堂的停车场可以当做直升机的临时机场,离施密特只有一英里。随着时间一分一秒的度过,安肖夫从一家跑到另一家,请求帮忙清理停车场,邻居们铲除自己的门前雪已经很累了,但都毫不犹豫地走出来。半个小时内,50多名自愿者在零度以下的寒风中清理停车场的积雪。

一名叫做基姆·费尔普斯的空服人员,也是飞机调度员,他为米歇尔调度了一架直升机送她从教堂去机场。教堂的空地可用作直升机起落,汉姆正忙着安排医疗队去教堂。

同时,芭芭拉电话告诉理尔喷气飞机驾驶员,詹森·史密斯,一定要准时在机场等候。像其他人一样,他和另一飞行员也被雪阻住了,但他表示一定能到达。一个警察和他的邻居开车送他们及时赶到机场。

最后,伴着暮色蜃景,WHAS广播公司派出一辆四轮车送米歇尔和她一家到教堂。当她们被推进仔细打扫干净的停车场时,那里

the meticulously cleared parking lot,there were 150 people,leaning on shovels,surrounded by mountainous piles of snow.As fire trucks arrived to provide makeshift landing lights for the helicopter,the crowd mushroomed to 300,applauding and waving as the Schmitts flew off into the snowy night.

Michelle's transplant was a success.It was the success not only of a skilled medical team,a child with the fight to survive and a family that wouldn't give up—but the success of a whole village that found something much better to do on January 17 than to stay warm inside and watch the snow.

CHICKEN SOUP

Susan G.Fey

有150个人拿着铁铲,周围是堆积如山的雪堆。当救火车赶到那儿充当直升机的着陆指示灯时,迅速聚集的人群已达300人,拍手目送施密特一家飞向雪夜。

米歇尔的移植手术非常成功,这成功不仅归功于医疗队精湛的医疗技术,也要归功于孩子的生存抗争和家人坚持不懈的努力。这成功更应归功于人们在1月17日那天没有选择待在家里取暖,观雪,而选择去做更有意义的事。

苏珊·G. 费

"Maybe you didn't notice, kid, but we have
a dress code here."

经 典 系 列／光 阴 的 故 事

What Courage Looks Like

I know what courage looks like.I saw it on a flight I took six years ago,and only now can I speak of it without tears filling my eyes at the memory.

When our L1011 left the Orlando airport that Friday morning,we were a chipper,high-energy group.The early-morning flight hosted mainly professional people going to Atlanta for a day or two of business.As I looked around,I saw lots of designer suits,CEO-caliber haircuts, leather briefcases and all the trimmings of seasoned business travelers.I settled back for some light reading and the brief flight ahead.

Immediately upon takeoff,it was clear that something was amiss. The aircraft was bumping up and down and jerking left to right.All the experienced travelers,including me,looked around with knowing grins. Our communal looks acknowledged to one another that we had experienced minor problems and disturbances before.If you fly much,you see these things and learn to act blasé about them.

We did not remain blasé for long.Minutes after we were airborne, our plane began dipping wildly and one wing lunged downward.The plane climbed higher but that didn't help.It didn't.The pilot soon made a grave announcement.

"We are having some difficulties," he said."At this time,it appears we have no nose-wheel steering.Our indicators show that our hydraulic system has failed.We will be returning to the Orlando airport at this time.Because of the lack of hydraulics,we are not sure our landing gear will lock,so the flight attendants will prepare you for a bumpy landing. Also,if you look out the airplane.We want to have as little on board as possible in the event of a rough touchdown."

双语精华版·心灵鸡汤·

何为勇气

　　我知道那是什么样的勇气，我在6年前的一次飞行中见识过。而且直到现在,6年后,我才能在提到它时,不再因回忆而热泪盈眶。

　　星期五上午当我乘坐的L1011号航班从奥兰多机场起飞时,我们这些乘客均兴致勃勃,早班飞机上搭乘的主要是去亚特兰大一至两天短期公务的职员。我往周围看了一看,大多是西装革履留着老板发式,带着皮革的公文包,全都是经验老到整洁干练的公务旅行者。我的旅程不长,坐在后排光线好的地方便于看书。

　　刚刚起飞,飞机就明显出了什么问题,上下左右的晃动。所有有经验的旅行者,包括我在内,均相互会心地一笑。我们的社会经验告诉我们遇到了一些小麻烦。如果你经常乘飞机,你就会明白是遇到气流了。

　　然而,我们遇到的不仅仅是气流,飞机才飞了几分钟开始急剧下坠,一侧机翼向下倾。飞机开始向上拉,但是没用,飞行员很快发布了危急通告。

　　"我们遇到了困难,"他说,"现在好像前轮失控。指示器显示压力系统失常,我们需返回奥兰多机场。因为没有压力系统,我们不能保证起落装置正常运行,飞机降落不稳,所以空乘服务员将帮助大家。另外,希望乘客在飞机冲撞地面时,不要从机舱往外看。"

In other words, we were about to crash. No sight has ever been so sobering as seeing that fuel, hundreds of gallons of it, streaming past my window out of the plane's tanks. The flight attendants helped people get into position and comforted those who were already hysterical.

As I looked at the faces of my fellow business travelers, I was stunned at the changes I saw in their faces. Many looked visibly frightened now. Even the most stoic looked grim and ashen. Yes, their faces actually looked gray in color, something I'd never seen before. There was not one exception. *No one faces death without fear,* I thought. Everyone lost composure in one way or another.

I began searching the crowd for one person who felt the peace and calm that true courage or great faith gives people in these events. I saw no one.

Then a couple of rows to my left, I heard a still, calm voice, a woman's voice, speaking in an absolutely normal conversational tone. There was no tremor or tension. It was a lovely, even tone. I had to find the source of this voice.

All around, people cried. Many wailed and screamed. A few of the men held onto their composure by gripping armrests and clenching teeth, but their fear was written all over them.

Although my faith kept me from hysteria, I could not have spoken so calmly, so sweetly at this moment as the assuring voice I heard. Finally, I saw her.

In the midst of all the chaos, a mother was talking, just talking, to her child. The woman, in her mid-30s and unremarkable looking in any other way, was staring full into the face of her daughter, who looked to be four years old. The child listened closely, sensing the importance of her mother's words. The mother's gaze held the child so fixed and intent that she seemed untouched by the sounds of grief and fear around her.

A picture flashed into my mind of another little girl who had recently survived a terrible plane crash. Speculation had it that she had

CHICKEN SOUP

换句话说,飞机可能会坠毁。而看到那些燃油,900加仑的油料从飞机巨大的油箱流经我们的窗下,现在的状况已算前所未有的冷静了。空乘服务员帮助每位乘客安置好,并且安抚那些惊吓过度的乘客。

当我看到和我同路的这些乘客的脸时,被他们脸上的变化惊呆了。许多人的脸上明显写着恐惧。甚至那些控制力极强的人的脸也是苍白而扭曲的。是的,他们的脸苍白,有些我以前从没见过的东西。无一例外,没有人面对死亡而不感到恐惧,所有的人都或多或少地失去了镇静。

我开始在人群中搜寻真正有勇气和意志的人,可以在这种状况下保持安宁和平静的人,但没有找到。

然而,我听到左边几排座位那边有一名妇女的声音依然非常平静,就像平时与人谈话的语调完全一样,没有颤抖,没有紧张,是非常可爱的,平和的语调,让我忍不住要去找声音的来源。环顾左右,人们哭喊着,许多人是哀号和尖叫,少数男人紧抓住扶手,咬紧牙关保持镇静,但浑身上下都表现出恐惧。

虽然,我的意志尚不至于让我疯狂,但我也不可能那么镇静。而我听到声音如此甜美,给人信心。我看到她了。

在这一片混乱中,一位母亲正对她的孩子讲话。这位女士外貌很平常,30岁左右,正凝视着她女儿的脸,小女孩看起来4岁左右,认真地听着、感觉到妈妈讲的话的重要性,妈妈的凝视让她安心,仿佛一点不受周围恐惧和悲痛的声音影响。

脑海中突然闪现出近期另一个空难中幸存的小女孩的画面。她之所以存活下来,主要是因为她的妈妈用自己的身体覆盖在她身上

lived because her mother had strapped her own body over the little girl's in order to protect her.The mother did not survive.The newspapers had been tracking how the little girl had been treated by psychologists for weeks afterward to ward off feelings of guilt and unworthiness that often haunt survivors.The child was told over and over again that it had not been her fault that her mommy had gone away.I hoped this situation would not end the same way.

I strained to hear what this mother was saying to her child.I was compelled to hear.I needed to hear.

Finally,I leaned over and by some miracle could hear this soft,sure voice with the tone of assurance.Over and over again,the mother said,"I love you so much.Do you know for sure that I love you more than anything?"

"Yes,Mommy," the little girl said.

"And remember,no matter what happens,that I love you always.And that you are a good girl.Sometimes things happen that are not your fault. You are still a good girl and my love will always be with you."

Then the mother put her body over her daughter's,strapped the seat belt over both of them and prepared to crash.

For no earthly reason,our landing gear held and our touchdown was not the tragedy it seemed destined to be.It was over in seconds.

The voice I heard that day never wavered,never acknowledged doubt,and maintained an evenness that seemed emotionally and physically impossible.Not one of us hardened business people could have spoken without a tremoring voice.Only the greatest courage,undergirded by even greater love,cold have borne that mother up and lifted her above the chaos around her.

That mom showed me what a real hero looks like.And for those few minutes,I heard the voice of courage.

Casey Hawley

保护她,而妈妈未能生还。报纸跟踪报道了小女孩怎样接受了心理医生几个星期的治疗,如其他幸存者经常发生的那样,这件事给她带来犯罪感和不值感。孩子一遍又一遍地重复说,妈妈的死,不是她的错。我真希望这样的状况不要再次发生。

我紧张地听着这位妈妈在对孩子说什么。我必须听,我需要听。

终于,我俯下身,很奇妙地听到了那语调镇定,温柔而又可信的声音。妈妈一遍遍地说:"我非常爱你,你一定要知道,我爱你胜过一切。"

"是的,妈妈,"小女孩说。

"要记住,无论发生了什么,妈妈始终爱你,你是个好孩子,无论发生什么都不是你的错,你始终是个好孩子,妈妈的爱一直和你在一起。"

然后,妈妈把身体俯在女儿身上,用座位上的安全带把她们一起捆住,准备经受飞机碰撞。

不知什么原因,起落装置很正常,飞机降落没有发生预期的碰撞,几秒钟后一切都过去了。

那天我听到的声音毫不颤动,没有一丝犹豫,非常的平静,这一切从生理上,从情感上来说都是不可能的,像我们这样坚毅的生意人也没有一个能毫不颤抖地说话, 只有怀有最大勇气的人才能做到。被博大的爱强化了的巨大勇气造就了这位母亲,使她凌驾于空难之上。

这位妈妈让我知道什么是真正的英雄。因为,在那几分钟,我听到了充满勇气的声音。

凯西·哈尔雷

The Power of a Promise

Laurie,my daughter,has always had three constants in her life from birth through her life's journey:her grandfather,her mother and one of her aunts.

In May of 1993,my father was diagnosed with terminal cancer and his prognosis was six to seven months.Laurie had applied to five universities across Canada to attend law school.In June,she was accepted at the University of Alberta in Edmonton,her first choice.

She went over to talk to her grandpa,telling him how she wasn't sure if she should move to Edmonton just then or if she should postpone the move for one year since he was ill.He looked her straight in the eye, shook his head no and said,"I want you to go to university in Edmonton.This is what you've worked for all these years.It is what you've always wanted for yourself and that is what I want for you."

She made her plans to move and before she left,she went to say good-bye to him.She said, "Grandpa,I don't want you to go anywhere while I'm gone.This can't be the last time I will see you or else I can't leave."He promised her that he would not go anywhere. "I'll be right here waiting for you when you get back," he said.My father was always a man of his word.

Laurie moved to Edmonton and started law school,while the rest of the family dealt with my father's illness day by day.Dad always accepted whatever life dealt him with good cheer and optimism.He was our

一诺千金

　　我的女儿劳拉从出世起，一直有3个人紧紧伴随着她：她的外公、妈妈和一个姑姑。

　　1993年5月，父亲被诊断为癌症晚期，医生诊断只有6~7个月的时间可活。此前，劳拉已向加拿大的5所大学的法律学院提出申请。7月，埃德蒙顿的阿尔伯塔大学接收了她，这是她的第一志愿。

　　她去征求外公的意见，因为外公有病，她拿不准是现在搬到埃德蒙顿去，还是推迟一年。外公直视着她的眼睛，摇摇头说："我想让你现在就搬到埃德蒙顿。这是你多少年努力奋斗的结果，是你自己的愿望，也是我对你的期望。"

　　于是她安排搬家。临行前，过来道别。她说："外公，我不在的期间，我不许你去任何地方。这绝不是我们最后一次见面，否则我就不走了。"外公答应她不去任何地方。"我会一直在这等你回来，"他安慰她说。我父亲向来是一诺千金的人。

　　劳拉搬到了埃德蒙顿，在法律学院读书。家里的其他人日夜照顾父亲。爸爸总是愉快、乐观地面对生活。他是大家的靠山，我们深

rock.We all depended on him so very much.Whenever we had a problem we went to Dad,and he was always there to give us encouragement and advice.

His health was failing rapidly and he prepared all of us for his ultimate death.He even made the plans for his own funeral to take the burden from us in our grief.

On November 29th,Dad asked us to take him to the hospital.He had developed a serious allergic reaction to one of the drugs he was taking, unknown to us at the time.He was very weak.A terrible rash covered his body and his skin had started to peel.The next several days,the whole family spent time at the hospital so that there would always be someone keeping him company.

CHICKEN SOUP

He was in terrible pain,yet he kept his good spirits.I specifically remember one Thursday night.He was sitting in a recliner chair between the two hospital beds.His eyes were closed,but he was aware of everything around him.Christmas music was playing on the television's weather channel.When "Winter Wonderland"came on,he started tapping his foot to the music.Christmas was one of his favorite seasons.

I had been in constant contact with Laurie about Dad's condition.I tried not to worry her too much because I wanted her to stay focused on her studies.She was aware of this,and in one phone conversation a few weeks earlier she had told me, "Mom,I don't want you just to call me when it is time to come home for Grandpa's funeral.I want to come home before that."

On Friday morning,I mentioned this conversation to one of my dad's doctors.He responded with, "You'd better call her today."That morning around 11:00,my dad was put on morphine and from then on, he never spoke again.

深地依赖他。出现问题时,就去找爸爸,他总会给我们帮助、鼓励和建议。

父亲的健康状况迅速恶化,他让我们准备后事,为了减轻我们的痛苦和负担,甚至安排好了自己的葬礼。

11月29日,爸爸让我们送他到医院。他对正在服用的一种药产生了严重的过敏反应,当时大家还蒙在鼓里。他非常虚弱,可怕的疹子布满全身,皮肤开始脱落。接下来的几天,家里所有的人都呆在医院,以便随时有人陪伴着他。

他十分痛苦,却仍保持乐观的天性。我尤其记得一个星期二的夜晚,他坐在两床之间的躺椅上,眼睛闭着,但却仍意识到周围发生的一切。圣诞音乐在天气频道播出,当"欢乐圣诞"乐曲响起,他的左脚随着音乐开始打拍子。圣诞是他最喜欢的时节。

我一直向劳拉通报爸爸的病情,也尽量不去烦扰她,让她集中精力学习。她意识到了,几周前一次通话时,她说:"妈妈,不要等到外公的葬礼时才告诉我,我想早点知道。"

星期五早晨,我把和劳拉的通话告诉了一位医生,他答道:"你最好今天就通知她。"那天早晨11点左右,爸爸被注射了吗啡。此后,他再也未开过口。

I tried to reach Laurie to tell her to come home as soon as possible, but she was at school.I kept calling but I couldn't reach her.I left messages asking her to phone me at the hospital as soon as she returned.By this time,we were at the hospital constantly.That evening,the night nurse informed us that Dad was in "transition",meaning he could pass away at any time.

CHICKEN SOUP

I was by Dad's bedside a lot,holding his hand or rubbing his feet because this soothed him.Around 1:00 A.M.,I noticed that his feet were cold and so were his legs,all the way up to his knees.His hands and arms were also cold,all the way up to his elbows.A short while later,my sister told me that she had tried to take his pulse but there didn't seem to be one.

Around 2:30 I got called to the phone—it was Laurie.I apprised her of the situation and told her the end was near.I said to her that he probably wouldn't live through the night.She asked me to please go back to Grandpa and tell him she would be on the first flight out in the morning,and that she would arrive in Winnipeg sometime near 10:00.She could be at the hospital between 10:30 and 11:00.I told her I didn't think I could do that because he had suffered enough,and I didn't want to prolong his agony,especially in his condition.She begged me. "Please, Mom,just go back and tell him what I said."

I went to Dad's bedside,took his hand,and told him that I'd just spoken with Laurie.I told him she was on her way back to Winnipeg on the earliest flight and that she would be at the hospital by 10:30,and that she wanted him to try to wait for her. Then I said, "Dad,if it's too painful for you to wait,it's okay. Laurie will understand."There was no response.I wasn't sure if he was even able to hear me,but then the strangest thing happened.

双语精华版·心灵鸡汤·

198

我一直打着电话,试图联系劳拉,告诉她尽可能早点回家,但她在上课,联系不上她。我留下了口信,让她一回来就给医院打电话找我。那天晚上,值夜班的护士通知我,爸爸处在"过渡期",意思是他随时都会去世。

我大部分时间坐在爸爸的床边,握着他的手或者摩擦他的脚,减轻他的痛苦。大约早晨1点,我发现他的脚变得冰凉,然后是腿,直到膝盖。手和胳臂也变冷了,直到肘部。过了一会,妹妹告诉我,她试图摸爸爸的脉搏,却没摸到。

两点半左右,接到了电话,是劳拉打来的。我告诉了她爸爸的情况,说一切都快结束了,很可能挺不过今天晚上。劳拉恳求我转告爸爸,她会乘早晨的第1趟航班出发,10点左右到达温尼伯,10点半至11点赶到医院。我告诉她,我想我做不到,爸爸已经遭受了足够的痛苦,不想再让他痛苦下去了,尤其现在的这种情况下。劳拉请求道:"求求你了,妈妈,你只管回去告诉他我说的话。"

来到爸爸的床边,握住他的手,告诉他我刚和劳拉通过话,劳拉正乘最早的航班,在赶往温尼伯的路上,大约10点半到达,劳拉想让他等她。我接着说:"爸爸,如果太痛苦了,就放弃吧。没有关系,劳拉会理解的。"爸爸没有反应。我不敢保证他是否听到了我的话,可接下来神奇的事情发生了。

I went back to his bedside and took his hand. It was warm. Yet from his wrist to his elbow, it was still cold! The same was true of his feet. They were warm, but his legs from his ankles to his knees were also still cold.

Laurie arrived at 10:35. I met her at the door to prepare her because she had not seen her Grandpa since she'd left in September. He had changed much in that time, especially in the past week.

She went to his side, took his hand and let him know she was there. She talked to him for about ten minutes and said her final farewell. He was actually gripping her hand as she spoke to him. Then, without letting go of her hand, he took one deep breath in and he was gone. It was 10:50 A.M..

Dad had kept his promise. He had waited for Laurie to get back before he went anywhere.

Dianne Demarcke

再回到他的床边,握起他的手,居然有了暖和气。然而,从腕部到肘部还是冰凉。脚也是一样,腿从脚踝到膝盖仍然很冰凉。

劳拉10点35分到的,自从9月离开后,从未见过外公。我到门口迎她,让她做好心理准备。她外公的变化太大了,尤其在最近的几个星期里。

劳拉来到床边,握起爸爸的手,让他知道她来了。劳拉喃喃地对他讲了大约10分钟,做最后的告别。当她说话时,爸爸实际上也在握着她的手。然后没有松手,只是深深地吐口气,才撒手人寰。时间是10点50分。

爸爸遵守了诺言,没有去任何地方,一直等着劳拉的到来。

戴安娜·德马克

经典系列／光阴的故事

Memories and Laughs

Two weeks before Des Moines Roosevelt's twentieth high-school reunion,I began frantically working out with arm and leg weights,shackled like an escapee from a prison chain gang.As I gyrated in the living room with my vintage Stevie Wonder album "Signed,Sealed,Delivered" going full blast,my children looked on in horror at my flying flesh. "Why are you doing that,Mommy?" they wondered.

"Because Mommy is silly and vain," I replied.Of course,two weeks didn't repair the ravages of the two decades since I last saw my classmates.I didn't go to the ten-year reunion—I was living out East then,and too hell-bent on my career to give a rip about auld lang syne.

But my regimen did give me the psychological boost I needed to face those people I worshipped and envied,despised and admired,and wept,dreamed and giggled with twenty years ago.I comforted myself that even if the reunion was miserable,it would make good copy.High school. How those two words dredge up a world of memories.

We were all carefully casual at first,our newly purchased stonewashed denim togs painstakingly ironed.But it soon came out that I wasn't the only one to indulge in useless preparations.

Several people succumbed to perms and crash diets.One woman confessed that she threw caution to the winds and baked like a lizard in the sun,on the theory that tanned fat looks better than pale.Forget the extra wrinkles she was creating for the thirty-year reunion.She wanted to look good now.

We all felt in our secret hearts that we were the only ones who hadn't changed appreciably.Naturally,we all went through the charade of

回忆与欢笑

离第蒙·罗斯福高中20年校友会还有两周时,我开始疯狂减肥。为减掉胳膊和腿上的赘肉,我把自己像监狱戴着锁链的囚犯一样绑起来,随着放到最大音量、我们那年代流行的史提夫·温德的唱片"限时专送,我爱你"的音乐在客厅旋转。孩子们惊恐地看着我飞转的身体,迷惑地问道:"妈妈,为什么这么做?"

"因为妈妈愚蠢,爱好虚荣。"我回答。当然,两周的时间无法补救20年的赘肉肆虐造成的灾难。已经20年没有见到同学了。10年聚会时我没有参加,因为当时搬离了东部,并过分地专注于事业,没太在乎往日的美好时光。

强化训练法并没有给我心理上的鼓舞,让我敢于面对这些20年前崇拜、嫉妒、鄙视、钦佩、哭泣、梦想和欢笑的人。我安慰自己,即使这次聚会再糟糕,也是值得的。高中,这两个字能挖掘出多少回忆啊!

开始时,大家都刻意装扮得随便一些,穿着新买的、精心熨过的磨砂粗斜纹布外套。不久就露馅了,我绝不是唯一一个花大力气进行徒劳准备的人。

好几个人烫了发,进行了速成节食。一个女同学坦白道,她把忠告抛到九霄云外,像蜥蜴一样在阳光下暴晒。她的理论是,晒成棕褐色的皮肤要比白花花的皮肤健康,根本不想这么做会为30年聚会造成更多的皱纹。她只想现在看起来漂亮。

大家内心深处都觉得,彼此肯定认不出来了。于是,顺理成章地拿着带名字的毕业照,进行一番仔细端详,试图把当初的歌唱明星

经典系列／光阴的故事

peering nearsightedly at name tags with graduation pictures on them,try-
ing to reconcile the track star with the paunch and then exclaiming
shamelessly,"You haven't changed a bit! "People were heard to mutter,
"My,this is strange."And more than one asked aloud,"Who are all these
old people?"

My claim to fame in those long-ago days was having the longest
hair in school,so several female classmates greeted me with the ac-
cusatory shriek,"You cut your hair! "Yes,ten years ago when it dawned
on me that strands of gray looked mighty peculiar in a waist-length
ponytail.

As I circulated,I learned that my fellow graduates include a colum-
nist for the New York Times,a neurologist on the faculty of Harvard
University Medical School and an actor-director whose first film won an
international award.Gee,why couldn't they have made something of
themselves.

As much pride as I took in hearing those classmates' accomplish-
ments,however, I must admit that a high point for me was visiting with
a woman who was once engaged to my former fiancé.We acted out
every man's worst nightmare as we compared notes,our victim merciful-
ly absent.If he could have walked in and seen us—wine glasses aloft,
heads thrown back,teeth bared as we screamed with laughter—he would
surely have turned tail and run.

The reunion held some other wonderful surprises,too.One was seeing a skinny boy who had worn thick glasses transformed with contact
lenses and confidence into a witty,gregarious CEO.The rest of him had
caught up with his Adam's apple,and he had married his highschool
sweetheart,a painfully shy girl who never communicated much except
for what shone out of her lovely eyes.Still soft-spoken but now self-
assured,she worked the room making everyone feel remembered and
unique.

与眼前这个大腹便便的家伙对上号来,接着毫不脸红地叫道:"你一点没变!"听到这话的人会嘟囔道:"哎呀,这就怪了。"还有不止一个人大声地问道:"这些老家伙是谁?"

在过去漫长的高中时期,长发让我校内闻名。所以,几个女同学见我打招呼时都是带着责备的尖叫:"你剪了头发!"是的,10年前我突然意识到,长及腰部、梳成马尾辫的灰发看起来很古怪。

随着与同学的交流,知道了同学中有一个是《纽约时报》的专栏作家,有一个是哈佛大学医学院的神经病学专家,有一个是导演,他导演的第一部电影获得了国际大奖。真是的,他们为什么不能有所作为呢?

听到同学们的成就,我非常骄傲。然而,必须承认我最得意的时刻是见到了曾经与我以前的未婚夫订婚的女同学。交谈中,我们把每个男人最见不得光的事情都抖搂出来,庆幸的是受害者没在场。如果他们走过来,看见我们觥筹交错,放浪形骸的样子,一定会立即转身逃之夭夭。

这次聚会的惊喜层出不穷。一个曾经戴着厚厚的眼镜,瘦得皮包骨似的男同学,现在脱胎换骨了。他戴着隐形眼睛,成了一位信心十足,聪明机智,左右逢源的CEO(执行总裁),身体也发福起来了。他和高中时的女友结了婚。当时,这个女孩极其害羞,从不与人交流,只有可爱的眼睛闪烁着善解人意的目光。现在,她说话仍柔声细语,却非常自信。整个屋子都活跃起来,每个人都觉得自己被惦念、与众不同起来。

Then there was the willowy girl whom we all expected to take the New York modeling scene by storm.She did,briefly,and is now back in Des Moines with six children,living happily ever after.

One of the school's most irrepressible boys (not major-league bad, just frequent-detention naughty) is now a probation officer. He told me that earlier in his career,when he worked with troubled youth,he challenged his charges to come up with an excuse he hadn't used himself.

And then there was the fellow who was legendary in grade school for his command of dirty words,now become a warmly friendly family man.He touched me by remembering the day I was introduced in kindergarten as the new girl,thirty-three years ago.

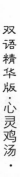

Of course,some things haven't changed.The homecoming queen was as ridiculously beautiful and unassuming as ever.And the class cynic lounged by the wall,owlishly observing,"Same old cliques."

Spouses looked on,eyes glassy with boredom and jaws aching from the effort of grinning at strangers as we classmates endlessly reminisced. My own beloved gave himself up to the indifferent canapés early on,and finally found a classmate's pregnant spouse who wanted to sit in a corner as desperately as he did.

Meanwhile,we Rough Riders remembered the time Diana's skirt fell off in the hall,and the time Jeff,on a dare,munched on a cow's eyeball during dissection in biology lab.

Between us,my five hundred classmates and I have survived bizarre religious cult experiences,drug experimentation,children,mortgages and a couple hundred divorces.We came from all over the world to take stock of ourselves and each other,and to remember the joys and insecurities of those wonderful,excruciating days.

We lifted a toast to those classmates who remain eternally young in our memories,claimed too soon by cancer,suicides and accidents.We are old enough now to know that we know very little—only that life is

有一个杨柳细腰的女同学,大家都预料到她会让纽约的模特行业大吃一惊。没用多长时间,她就做到了。现在带着6个孩子回到第蒙·罗斯福高中,要安度余生了。

一个曾经是学校里最难管束的男同学（不是捣蛋分子中的头儿,只是经常淘气挨留而已）,现在成了监督缓刑犯的官员。他告诉我,刚开始做这个与问题青年打交道的工作时,质疑过自己的工作,因为现在的青年鬼点子很多,经常让自己穷于应付。

有一个家伙,因为使用脏字炉火纯青,在小学就是家喻户晓的人物。现在变成了一个温文尔雅的居家好男人。他还记得33年前我进幼儿园的情景,让我很感动。

当然,有些事情没有变化。聚会的女王仍像以前一样美丽大方得让人捧腹大笑。班级的愤世嫉俗者仍懒洋洋地靠在墙边,神情严肃地观察着,"还是以前的帮派作风"。

当大家没完没了地叙旧时,家属们旁观着,无聊让眼睛失去神采,对陌生人强挤的笑容让双腮酸胀。我家那位从来这儿开始,就一直投身于饮食。酒足饭饱后,发现一位同学怀有身孕的伴侣和他一样绝望地躲坐在角落里。

我们这些"莽骑兵"还记得戴安娜的裙子掉落在礼堂里的情景,还记得在生物实验室的解剖课上,杰夫胆大包天、嚼牛眼睛的情景。

500名校友和我一起经历了怪异的宗教狂热运动、毒品、孩子、房屋抵押和几百次的离异。我们来自世界各地,评判自己,评判他人,回忆着美妙却苦楚的岁月里的那些欢笑和不安。

我们举杯向那些记忆中永葆青春,却过早地被癌症、自杀和意外夺去生命的同学致敬。我们已久历沧桑,知道自己的渺小,却深刻

short,and we must all try to be good to one another.

All in all,I'm awfully glad I went,and awfully glad my arms can go back to jelly now.My only regret is that not a single cheerleader had gotten fat!

Rebecca Christian

CHICKEN SOUP

地知道人生短暂,要尽自己所能善待他人。

总之,我十分高兴参加了聚会,十分高兴现在胳臂可以恢复成肉卷了。唯一的遗憾是,没有一个拉拉队队长变胖!

丽贝卡·克里斯汀

THE FAMILY CIRCUS® By Bil Keane

"I need a hug, Mommy. I
used up the last one."

经典系列／光阴的故事

Innocence Abroad

Fate loves the fearless.

James Russell Lowell

My wife prepared breakfast as I stood at the dining room window gazing beyond a sentinel row of palm trees at the early morning sun forcing its rays through wisps of Texas fog.Our three-year-old daughter, Becky,was in the backyard,her attention riveted to the antics of a pair of quarreling blue jays.

Suddenly I snapped to attention.An awesome creature,ugly and misshapen,was meandering up the alley.In the hazy light of the early morning,it appeared like a monster out of the past.It was a huge thing, armed with long,curving tusks;down its high,arched back ran a great ridge,crowned with stiff bristles.I realized suddenly what it was:a pugnacious javelina,the fierce,wild hog of the Southwest plains country.

I took no time to ponder where it came from or how it had managed to penetrate a thickly populated residential section,for it was progressing slowly,grunting,sniffing and rooting with its long snout as it ambled along.I started to shout to Becky to run inside,but I was too late. She and the animal had sighted each other simultaneously.The grunting shifted to a low,menacing rumble.The tip of the long nose was an inch from the ground,gleaming button eyes were fastened on my daughter,the beast's four stubby legs were braced to charge.

I started to dash upstairs for a gun,but I knew I could never get it in time.As though hypnotized,I stared at the drama that was unfolding just a few yards away.

无知者无畏

命运偏爱勇敢者。

詹姆斯·拉塞尔·洛厄尔

我妻子做早饭的时候，我站在餐厅的窗户那儿从一排整齐的棕榈树上方向外看，清晨的阳光透过得克萨斯州的晨雾照射着后院，我们3岁的女儿贝基，正在那儿全神贯注地观察一对蓝色的樫鸟打架。

突然，我发现一只可怕的动物，畸形又丑陋，正往小路上靠过来，在清早朦胧的光线中，它就像故事中提到的妖怪，身形巨大，青面獠牙，蹲身拱背地跑过山梁，身上长满了鬃毛。我突然意识到，那是一只凶猛好斗的西南平原地区的野猪。

我没有时间考虑它从哪里来，它是怎样穿过人口稠密的住宅区到这儿来的，它正一边哼哼着，一边抽着鼻子，长嘴拱地，慢慢前行。我开始喊叫贝基走开，但是太迟了，她和那只动物已经互相看见对方了。野猪的声音变得很低沉，恐吓地哼哼着。长鼻子的前端离地只有1英寸，两只发光的扣子眼紧盯着我的女儿，4条树桩似的腿绷得笔直，摆出一副进攻的架势。

我想冲上楼去拿枪，但我知道来不及了。像被催眠了似的，只能紧紧盯着几米远处发生的事件。

Becky approached the javelina,hands outstretched,making gurgling childish sounds as she advanced.The hog stood its ground,its grunts even more threatening.I looked at those fearsome tusks and the sharp even teeth—one slash could lay a man open.

I started to call to my wife,but something held me mute.If she should look out the window and scream,a chain reaction might be touched off that could end in terrible tragedy.

Becky,who had been only a few steps away from the beast when they first sighted each other,closed the distance between them with calm deliberation.With hands still outstretched,she reached the side of the beast.One small hand went up to a tough,bristly ear and scratched it.The deep-throated rumblings gradually turned into a gravely,almost purring sound.I thought irrelevantly of the idling of a powerful motor.The top of the round,wet nose was gently nudging against Becky's ankle.Unbelievably,the animal seemed to be enjoying the attention he was receiving, and my pulse beat slowly dropped to normal.Some perception within the ugly creature must have told him that he had nothing to fear from this tiny child.

The encounter ended as abruptly as it began.Becky suddenly turned away and came toward the house.The javelina seemed to realize that the short love fest was over and slowly ambled on its way.

Becky passed me as she came through the room."Nice doggie,Daddy," she said nonchalantly.

Henry N.Ferguson

贝基接近野猪,一边前行,一边张开手,口中发出孩子的喃喃声。野猪站在那儿,嗯嗯地叫得更加可怕。我看着它令人恐怖的獠牙,非常锋利,足以刺穿人体。

　　我想喊妻子,但又不敢。如果她从窗户向外看并尖叫起来,未免会引起连锁反应,后果将不堪设想。

　　当贝基第一眼看到野猪时,他们之间只有几步远,现在离得越来越近了。贝基和那野兽好像都在思考。小手依然张开着,贝基走到野猪身边,一只小手去抓它的坚硬有硬毛的耳朵。野猪从喉中发出的低沉的嗯嗯声渐渐变成响亮的欢快的呜呜声,让人联想到空转的大功率发动机。野猪圆圆的湿漉漉的鼻子轻轻地拱着贝基的脚踝。令人难以置信,那家伙仿佛很喜欢别人对它的关注。我的脉搏跳动开始放慢到正常频率。这个丑陋的动物可能感知到,这个小小的孩子不会伤害到它。

　　这件事如它突然发生那样,突然结束了。贝基忽然转头向房子这儿走过来。野猪好像也认识到短暂的爱抚结束了,于是慢慢地走开了。

　　贝基在走向房间经过我身边时,只是淡淡地说:"好可爱的小狗狗,爸爸。"

亨利·N. 弗格森

Write Your Own Life

> *Whatever the mind can conceive and believe it can achieve.*
>
> Napoleon Hill

Suppose someone gave you a pen—a sealed,solid-colored pen.

You couldn't see how much ink it had.It might run dry after the first few tentative words or last just long enough to create a masterpiece (or several) that would last forever and make a difference in the scheme of things.You don't know before you begin.

Under the rules of the game,you really never know.You have to take a chance!

Actually,no rule of the game states you must do anything. Instead of picking up and using the pen,you could leave it on a shelf or in a drawer where it will dry up,unused.

But if you do decide to use it,what would you do with it?How would you play the game?

Would you plan and plan before you ever wrote a word?Would your plans be so extensive that you never even got to the writing?

Or would you take the pen in hand,plunge right in and just do it, struggling to keep up with the twists and turns of the torrents of words that take you where they take you?

双语精华版·心灵鸡汤·

书写自己的人生

人的头脑所能构思而确信的,人便能完成它。

拿破仑·希尔

假设有人给你一支笔,一支单色的、不可拆卸的笔。

看不见有多少墨水,也许写上几笔,墨水就会用尽。也许能用很长时间,足以写出一部(或几部)惊天传世之作。在开始前,一切都是未知。

这就是游戏规则,一切都是未知。你必须抓住机会!

事实上,没有游戏规则告诉你该做什么。除了拿起笔,使用它,还可以把它弃置于书架、抽屉之中,任其墨干。

一旦决定用它,怎么用呢?怎么进行这场游戏?

是思忖良久,才动笔写作呢?还是思绪万千,无从下手呢?

是握笔在手,全然投入,任辞藻滔滔不绝,千回百转,一直前行呢?

Would you write cautiously and carefully, as if the pen might run dry the next moment, or would you pretend or believe (or pretend to believe) that the pen will write forever and proceed accordingly?

And of what would you write: Of love? Hate? Fun? Misery? Life? Death? Nothing? Everything?

Would you write to please just yourself? Or others? Or yourself by writing for others?

Would your strokes be tremblingly timid or brilliantly bold? Fancy with a flourish or plain?

Would you even write? Once you have the pen, no rule says you have to write. Would you sketch? Scribble? Doodle or draw?

Would you stay in or on the lines, or see no lines at all, even if they were there? Or are they?

There's a lot to think about here, isn't there?

Now, suppose someone gave you a life⋯.

David A. Berman

是因担心墨水会随时枯竭而谨小慎微呢？还是想当然或者确信（或者想当然地确信）墨水会用之不尽而尽情使用呢？

写什么呢？爱情？仇恨？趣闻？苦难？生活？死亡？什么都写？什么都不写？

是为取悦自己而写呢？还是为取悦他人而写呢？还是通过为他人而写取悦自己呢？

笔锋是胆怯懦弱，还是粗犷豪放？是炫耀粉饰，还是简单朴实？

是不是要写呢？有了笔，可没有规则说必须写。是素描？是乱写乱画？是漫不经心的乱涂，还是细心的绘制？

是在行间书写呢？是在行上书写呢？还是即使有行，却视而不见呢？这些真的是行吗？

需要思考的很多，很多，对吗？

现在，假设有人给了你人生……

大卫·A. 伯曼

Angels Never Say "Hello!"

My grandma told me about angels.She said they come knocking at the door of our hearts,trying to deliver a message to us.I saw them in my mind's eye with a big mail sack slung between their wings and a post office cap set jauntily on their head.I wondered if the stamps on their letters said"Heaven Express."

"No use waiting for the angel to open your door," Grandma explained. "You see,there is only one door handle on the door of your heart.Only one bolt.They are on the in side.Your side.You must listen for the angel,throw open the lock and open up that door! "

I loved the story and asked her again and again to tell me, "What does the angel do then? "

"The angel never says 'hello'.You reach out and take the message,and the angel gives you your instructions: 'Arise and go forth! ' Then the angel flies away.It is your responsibility to take action."

When I am interviewed by the media,I am often asked how I have built several international businesses without any college education, beginning my business on foot,pushing my two children before me in a dilapidated baby stroller with a wheel that kept coming off.

First I tell the interviewers that I read at least six books a week, and have done so since I was able to read.I hear the voices of all the great achievers in their books.

Next,I explain that every time I hear an angel knock,I just fling open the door.The angel's messages are about new business ideas,books to write and wonderful solutions to problems in my career and personal life.They come very often,in a never-ending flow,a river of ideas.

天使总会不期而至

奶奶告诉过我天使的故事。她说,天使来时会敲打我们的心灵之门,传递天使之音。在我的脑海中,天使的翅膀间挂着大大的邮包,头上戴着神气的邮帽。我不禁好奇,它们的邮票是否写着"天堂快递"。

"等待天使打开你的门是徒劳的,"奶奶解释说,"你看,心灵之门只有一个把手,一个门闩,却在门里面,在你的这面。你必须仔细倾听天使的到来,打开门锁,推开心灵之门!"

我喜欢这个故事,一遍又一遍地让她给我讲。"天使进来后做什么?"

"天使从不说'你好'。你伸出手就会得到天使的音信,天使发出指示:'起来,前进!'说完,天使就飞走了。你的责任就是按照天使的指示采取行动。"

媒体采访我时经常问到,没有大学背景,白手起家,推着一个破旧的、经常掉轮子的婴儿车,带着两个孩子,是怎么建立起一个国际大公司的。

首先,我告诉他们,从会识字开始,每星期读6本书。在书中,听到了那些伟人的声音。

其次,我解释说,每次听到天使敲门时,我就把门敞开。天使的音信源源不断;纷至沓来,有关于新创意的,关于新书的,关于事业和个人生活中绝好的解决办法的。

However, there was one time when the knocking stopped. It happened when my daughter, Lilly, was badly hurt in an accident. She was riding on the back of a forklift her father rented to move some hay for our horses. Lilly and two of the neighbor children begged him to let them ride on the forklift when he took it back to the rental place.

Going down a little hill, the steering gear broke. Her father almost pulled his arms out of their sockets trying to hold the big rig on the road before it turned over. The little neighbor girl broke her arm. Lilly's father was knocked unconscious. Lilly was pinned underneath, with the huge weight of the rig on her left hand. Gasoline spilled on her thigh. Gasoline burns, even if it is not ignited. The neighbor boy was unhurt and kept his wits. He ran out and stopped traffic.

We rushed Lilly to Orthopedic Hospital where they began a long series of operations, each time amputating more of her hand. They told me that when a human limb is cut off, sometimes it can be sewn back on, but not if it is smashed and crushed.

Lilly had just started piano lessons. Because I am a writer, I had looked forward with great anticipation to her taking typing lessons the next year.

During this time I often drove off by myself to cry, not wanting others to see me. I couldn't stop. I found I did not have the concentration to read anything. No angels knocked. There was a heavy silence in my heart. I kept thinking of all the things Lilly would never do because of this terrible accident.

When we took her back to the hospital for the eighth amputation, my spirit was very low. I kept thinking over and over, "She will never type! Never type. Never type."

We set her bag down in the hospital room and suddenly turned around because a young teenage girl in the next bed said to us in a commanding voice: "I've been waiting for you! You go down the hall

然而,有一段时间,天使的敲门声停了。这是在我的女儿莉莉车祸严重受伤的期间。当他爸爸把租来给马运草料的铲车送回租借公司时,莉莉和两个邻居家的孩子央求他让他们坐在铲车上。于是,她坐在了铲车的后面。

下山时,铲车的转向装置坏了,他爸爸竭尽全力试图控制住车。车还是翻了,邻居家的女孩折断了胳膊,莉莉的爸爸被撞得失去知觉,莉莉被压在车下,大车架死死地压住她的左胳臂。汽油流淌在她的大腿上。不需要点燃,汽油就着了。邻居家的男孩没有受伤,还保持着理智,跑出来,拦住了车。

我们飞快地把莉莉送到矫形医院,做了一系列的手术。每次都会截去她手的一部分。医生们告诉我,人的四肢被切除后还可以再缝合复原,条件是四肢未被碾碎。

莉莉刚好开始学钢琴课。因为自己是个作家的原因,我非常期望她第2年学习打字课程。

这段时间,我常常独自开车到无人的僻静之处,偷偷地哭泣。我难以自持,发现自己再不能集中精神读任何东西。天使也不敲门了。我心事重重,常想到因为这场车祸,莉莉永远也不能做事情。

我们送她到医院做第8次截肢的时候,我精神沮丧,总是不停地想:"她永远不能打字了! 永远不能了。永远不能了。"

把她的包刚放到病房里,我转过身来,因为突然听到隔壁的床上一个十来岁的小女孩以命令的口气说:"我等你们好长时间了!现

right now, third room on the left! There is a boy there who was hurt in a motorcycle accident. You go down there and lift up his spirit, right now!"

She had the voice of a field marshal. We immediately obeyed her. We talked to the boy and encouraged him, and then came back to Lilly's hospital room.

For the first time I noticed that this unusual girl was bent way over. "Who are you?" I asked.

"My name is Tony Daniels," she grinned. "I go to the handicapped high school. This time the doctors are going to make me a whole inch taller! You see, I had polio. I have had many operations."

She had the charisma and strength of a General Schwartzkopf. I couldn't help the words that came flying out of my mouth. I gasped, "But you aren't handicapped!"

"Oh, yes, you are right," she replied, looking sideways at me. "They teach us down at our school that we are never handicapped as long as we can help someone else. Now, if you met my schoolmate who teaches the typing class, you might think she is handicapped because she was born with no arms and no legs. But she helps all of us by teaching us typing, with a wand between her teeth."

Ka bang! Suddenly I heard it—the clanging noise of pounding and kicking and yelling at the door of my heart!

I ran out of the room and down the corridor to find a pay phone. I called IBM and asked for the office manager. I told him my little girl had lost nearly all of her left hand, and asked him if they had one-hand touch-typing charts.

He replied, "Yes, we do! We have charts for the right hand, the left hand, charts that show how to use your feet with pedals, and even to type with a wand between your teeth. The charts are free. Where would you like me to send them?"

CHICKEN SOUP

在立刻沿着走廊到左边的第3个房间去！那里有一个在摩托车肇事中受伤的男孩子,去那里让他振作起来。立刻就去！"

她说话的口气像元帅,让我们不得不马上按照她的话行动。跟小男孩谈心,鼓励他之后,我回到了莉莉的病房。

第1次, 我注意到, 这个不同寻常的孩子浑身蜷曲着。"你是谁？"我问。

"我叫托尼·丹尼尔斯,"她笑着回答,"我是残疾高中的学生。这次,医生要让我整整长高一寸！你看见了,我得的是小儿麻痹。我做过许多手术。"

她有着施瓦茨科普夫将军般的魅力和威严。我惊叹着,禁不住脱口而出:"你好好的呀！"

"哦,是的,没错。"她斜视着我回答,"学校教育我们,只要能自立,就不是残疾。现在,如果见到教我们打字的校友,你也许会认为她有残疾,因为她生来就没有四肢。但是现在她能帮助所有的人,口中咬着打字棒,教我们打字。"

当当！突然,我听到了它——那敲打我心灵之门的声音:拍打声,踢踏声和叫喊声。

我迅速跑出了病房,沿走廊找到了电话,给IBM公司打电话找经理。告诉他我的女儿失去了整只右手,问他是否有单手打字图示。

他回答道:"有,我们有！我们有右手的,左手的,脚的,甚至口中叼棒的。这些图示都是免费的。需要我寄给你吗？"

CHICKEN SOUP

When we were finally able to take Lilly back to school, I took the one-hand typing charts with me. Her hand and arm were still in a cast with big bandages around it. I asked the school principal if Lilly could take typing, even though she was too young, instead of gym. He told me it had never been done before, and that perhaps the typing teacher would not want to go to the extra trouble, but I could ask him if I wanted to.

When I stepped into the typing class I noticed immediately that all around the room were signs with quotations from Florence Nightingale, Ben Franklin, Ralph Waldo Emerson and Winston Churchill. I took a deep breath, realizing I was in the right place. The teacher said he had never taught one-hand typing before but that he would work with Lilly every lunch period. "We will learn one-hand touch-typing together."

Soon Lilly touch-typed all of her homework for her English class. Her English teacher that year was a polio victim. His right arm hung helplessly by his side. He scolded her, "Your mother is babying you, Lilly. You have a good right hand. You do your own homework."

"Oh, no sir." She smiled at him. "I'm up to 50 words a minute one-handed in my touch-typing. I have the one-hand IBM charts！ "

The English teacher sat down suddenly. Then he said slowly, "Being able to type has always been my dream."

"Come on over during lunchtime. The back of my charts have the other hand. I'll teach you！ " Lilly told him.

It was after the first lunchtime lesson that she came home and said, "Mama, Tony Daniels was right. I'm not handicapped anymore, because I am helping someone else fulfill his dream."

Today, Lilly is the author of two internationally acclaimed books. She has taught all of our office staff to use our Apple computers with our mouse pad on the left side, because that is where she makes hers fly around with her remaining finger and the stump of her thumb.

Shush. Listen！ Do you hear the knocking? Throw the bolt！ Open the door！ Please think of me and remember：Angels never say"hello." Their greeting is always"Arise and go forth！ "

Dottie Walters

最终，送莉莉回学校时，我随身带着单手打字图示。她的胳臂打着石膏，缠着绷带。我问校长莉莉虽然年龄小点，可不可以上打字课，而不上体操课。他回答说，这没有过先例，也许打字老师不愿意添上这种额外的麻烦，但是可以去问问打字老师。

我走进打字教室，注意到到处都是弗劳伦斯·南丁格尔、本·弗兰克林、拉尔夫·沃尔多·爱默生和温斯顿·丘吉尔的名言。我长舒了口气，知道来对了地方。老师说，他以前从未教过单手打字，但是他愿意在午休时间一起尝试一下："我们一起学习单手打字吧。"

不久，莉莉可以打字做英语作业了。英语老师是个小儿麻痹的受害者，右臂无助地吊在一边，他批评道："你妈妈把你惯坏了，莉莉。你的右胳臂还健在，你可以自己做作业。"

"噢，不，先生。"她冲他笑着说，"我单手打字最多可以打50个词。我有IBM单手打字图示。"

英语教师颓然坐下，然后慢慢说："能够打字一直是我的梦想。"

"午休时过来，我的图示后面有右手的，我教你。"

第1次午休课回家后，她说："妈妈，托尼·丹尼尔斯说得对。我不再残疾，因为我帮助他人实现了自己的梦想。"

今天，莉莉写两本书已经闻名世界。她教会我们公司的职员使用左手鼠标垫的苹果电脑，因为那就是她残余的手，一展身手的地方。

安静，听！听到敲门声了吗？拉开门闩！打开心灵之门！请记着我和我说的话：天使从不说"你好。"他们的问候总是"起来，前进！"

多蒂·沃尔特斯

A Match Made in Heaven

There is nothing the body suffers that the soul may not profit by.

George Merideth

I scrubbed and gowned while my OB-GYN colleague explained the situation to me.A first-time mother carrying twins had gone into labor three months before her due date,all attempts to stop the labor had failed.As I entered the delivery room I noticed the father tenderly supporting his wife while she prepared for the delivery.

The obstetrician looked up at me strangely,then handed me an object as the father looked on.It was a tiny arm.Within seconds out came Twin A,crying and noticeably premature.I quickly took the baby to the bassinet,gave him oxygen and assessed his status.He was working to breathe.I was certain that with this degree of prematurity he would suffer hyaline membrane (a lung disease affecting premature infants).I left Twin A with a nurse and returned to receive Twin B,also vigorously crying.The only obvious deficiency was the absence of his left arm.

The twins were taken to the neonatal nursery.Chest X rays revealed moderately severe premature lung disease,requiring high oxygen support. After the twins had been stabilized,I finally had a chance to talk with the parents,Mr.and Mrs.Arnold.We discussed premature lung disease and the potential complications,and how the first forty-eight hours were very critical in their care and prognosis.Then I addressed the issue of the absent left arm.

I explained that when an appendage of the baby in utero pokes

天生一对

身体上的痛苦就是灵魂上的收获。

乔治·梅里迪斯

　　做术前准备时,妇产科的同事向我介绍了情况。这位妇女是首次生产。怀了双胞胎,而且比预产期提前3个月,所有阻止分娩的努力都失败了。走进分娩室,就看见丈夫正温柔地安抚着在做分娩前准备的妻子。

　　因为丈夫在一旁观看,产科医生只能用奇怪的眼神看了我一眼,然后递给我一样东西。这是一只细小的胳臂。几秒后,双胞胎的老大出来了。显然是早产儿,费力地呼着气。我快速地把他放到摇篮里,给他吸氧,评估他的状况。我敢确定,这种程度的早产儿会得新生儿肺透明膜病(一种早产儿患的肺部疾病)。我把老大留给护士照看,返回去接双胞胎的老二,他也在大声地哭着。老二有一个缺陷,没有左胳膊。

　　双胞胎被送到育婴室。胸透表明,他们患有中等程度的早产儿肺部疾病,需要大量吸氧。稳定后,我终于有机会和他们的父母阿诺德夫妇谈话。我告诉他们早产儿肺部疾病以及潜在的复杂情况,尤其是头48小时对于治疗和诊断至关重要。接着,告诉他们孩子没有胳臂的事情。

　　我解释说,当母体内婴儿的肢体穿透包在他身上正在发育的膜

through a developing membrane surrounding the baby,the membrane closes back again,amputating the limb or digit.The Arnolds' responses to these grave conditions were full of hope,and I was struck by their strength of character.They remained strong through the next several days,lovingly encouraging their twins,Mathew and Jonathan,as the babies suffered complications.

CHICKEN SOUP

The twins responded well.It was a joy to see them finally go home without any residual effects from their premature birth,such as permanent lung disease or brain damage.The Arnolds continued their dedication to their children,immediately exploring different prosthetic options for Mathew.Mrs.Arnold phoned and researched many sources to find out when and how a prosthesis should be utilized with a growing child.She read voraciously.She made contacts all over the world,trying to find the most knowledgeable individuals to help Mathew.It was an honor to witness this mother's love,trying to solve this child's special challenge.

Two years later our family moved to the Midwest,but Mrs.Arnold still kept me up to date on Mathew's progress.About ten years later, while I was working as a pediatric radiologist at a children's hospital,I met the Sanders.They had just adopted a six-month-old infant from Korea.Baby Billy had a swollen elbow,the result of a tumor in the elbow joint of the right arm.A biopsy revealed a malignancy,and because of the extensive involvement of the joint and bone,amputation above the elbow was the only possibility for complete cure.

Once again I witnessed the love and fortitude of caring parents. Right away,Mrs.Sanders set out to find all about the prosthetic devices.I knew Mrs.Arnold had thoroughly investigated this problem.It was an easy connection to make.The two mothers communicated by phone and by letter,and I know their connection became a tremendous support for both families.

Later,I learned that young Mathew began to write Billy encouraging

时，膜会重新封闭，从而切断肢体或手指。面对这种严峻形势，阿诺德夫妇的回答却让人释然，他们坚强的性格深深感染了我。在接下来的几天中，当婴儿——马修和乔纳森病情危急的时候，他们也一直很坚强，对婴儿充满怜爱和希望。

双胞胎进展良好。看见他们没有患任何早产儿肺部疾病或者脑部损伤等后遗症，大家都非常高兴。阿诺德夫妇对孩子的关怀并没有停止，立即就探讨为马修做修复手术的事情。阿诺德夫人打电话咨询了很多人，查阅了许多资料，想了解新生儿修复术合适的时间和方法。她废寝忘食地阅读相关资料，联系了各个地方，试图找到有最渊博学识的人帮助马修。目睹这位母亲的爱和她为迎接孩子特殊的挑战所做的努力，我们充满敬意。

两年后，我家搬到了中西部地区，可阿诺德夫人仍向我通报马修最新的进展情况。10年后，我在一家儿童医院当儿科放射学医生，遇到了桑德斯夫妇，他们刚从韩国领养了一个6个月大的婴儿比利，他右臂肘关节患有肿瘤，肘部肿大。病理切片表明是恶性肿瘤。因为连接大量关节和骨骼，肘部以上截肢是彻底治愈的唯一选择。

我又一次目睹了父母护理孩子过程中表现出来的执著的爱和他们坚强的性格。术后不久，桑德斯夫人就动手寻找所有的修复仪器。我知道阿诺德夫人曾对修复仪器进行过深入的研究，很快联系上了她。两位母亲通过电话和书信交流。我深知，这种交流是两个家庭强有力的支柱。

后来，我了解到小马修开始给比利写信鼓励他。马修变成了一

letters.Mathew had become an outstanding young man,both academically and athletically.He participated in all sports,and excelled in basketball and soccer.In his letters,Mathew offered Billy helpful tips on shoe tying and tree climbing,and ways to respond to public stares.As Billy got older,Mathew became a very important role model.

One summer when Billy was five years old and Mathew was fifteen,the Arnolds took a crosscountry vacation,which brought them through our city.We held a three-family picnic in our backyard.It was touching to see young Billy meet Mathew,his longtime hero and role model.I saw Billy on the sideline,awestruck as he watched Mathew play basketball,and I could almost see the wheels turning in his head:"Wow, if he can do that with one arm…"

At the end of the day,we were all sitting around the picnic table and I was saying what a blessing it was for the families to have found each other,and for Billy to have come to know Mathew.It was clear to me that problems surrounded by love become blessings that reap more of the same.

As we were talking,everyone noticed that Billy's and Mathew's absent arms were side by side.Billy looked around at everybody and said,"Yep,I guess we're a match made in heaven."

Everyone laughed—with tears in our eyes.

James C.Brown,M.D.

个学习和体育都非常出色的年轻人，参加了所有的体育活动，尤其擅长篮球和足球。在他的信中，对系鞋带、爬树和如何面对别人的目光等问题，向比利提出了有益的建议。伴随着比利的成长，马修成为了他的效仿榜样。

比利5岁、马修15岁的这年夏天，阿诺德一家利用假期进行了一次全国旅行，正好来到我所在的城市。在我家的后院，我们举行了一次有3家参加的野餐会。看见比利见到马修——他多年的偶像和榜样——的情景，大家都很感慨。比利站在边线上，充满崇敬地看着马修打篮球，不难想象他的小脑瓜里转着什么想法："哇，他居然能用一支胳臂打篮球……"

野餐结束时，大家坐在桌旁。我说，你们两家碰面，比利亲眼见到了马修，这是多么高兴的事情啊！这件事对我的启迪是，如果缺陷被爱包围，它就变成了一种祝福，会收获更多的祝福。

大家聊天时都注意到比利和马修两个残缺的肩紧紧地靠在一起。比利环视一周，说道："你看，我们是天生的一对。"

大家都笑了，每个人眼里都充满了喜悦的泪水。

詹姆斯·C. 布朗，医学博士